A Children's Story

Written by Rosen Trevithick

And Illustrated by Katie W. Stewart

Suitable for independent reading by children aged 8-10.

Ideal for reading aloud to younger children.

First Edition

Text copyright Rosen Trevithick, 2013

Illustrations copyright Katie W. Stewart, 2013

All Rights Reserved

Thanks to TextMender Editing Services

www.textmender.com

For Reuben and Sebastian

Prologue

The little girl looked very tasty. Her pigtails, tied with little pink bows, were like sugar sprinkles to a troll, and this troll had a very sweet tooth indeed. He licked his lips feeling optimistic about his chances.

He was bigger than the little girl – twice as tall and three times as wide. He was much stronger than her, with arms so round that they looked like two sausage dogs dangling from his shoulders. He was scarier than she was, with sharp teeth and yellow eyes. He was hungrier than she was, with a rumbling stomach and green saliva dripping from his mouth. However, the one thing that the troll didn't have was a very big brain.

He gazed across the river from behind a

tree, as the little girl skipped and sang to herself in a very appetising manner. He knew that he couldn't swim, but he wouldn't let the river stand in his way. A knobbly green crocodile cruised past. The troll ignored it; he was too busy thinking about his dinner.

"I know," thought the troll, "if I be reaching my arms out like a plane, and then I be running fast, I be flying over the river."

What the troll didn't know was that aeroplanes are aerodynamic. They are smooth and slender to make flying easy. If there's one thing that is not aerodynamic, it's a troll. The troll was built like a giant potato stuffed with rocks.

He took a step backwards and held out his big, fat, sausage dog arms. Using all the energy he could muster, he pushed forward. "Zoom!" he cried, imagining he was a jet plane. Instead, he waddled like a duck and promptly plopped into the river.

The little girl heard an almighty splash. She turned to see what had caused it. At first, she saw nothing. However, a few moments later, she noticed a very happy crocodile licking his lips.

She went back to skipping, unaware that she had once been on a troll's dinner menu. In fact, like most little girls, she had no idea that trolls really exist. But of course, trolls do exist. They are very real indeed.

Rosen Trevithick

Chapter 1

The Boy Who Knew About Real Trolls

Rufus Sebbleford was a very special boy. He was the only boy in the whole world who knew about real trolls. And the reason that he was the only boy in the world who knew about real trolls, was that he was the only boy who had ever seen one. He was five years, three-hundred and sixty-four days old when it happened.

It was the night before his sixth birthday. Rufus was a skinny boy with bright red hair and shiny blue eyes that matched his Thomas the Tank Engine pyjamas. He lay in bed far too excited for sleep. Every other boy in Sludgeside was sound asleep, but not Rufus.

He was just wondering whether his

birthday presents would include a new ladder for his den, when suddenly the room went totally dark. Something blocked the moonlight from shining through the thin silver curtains – something big and built like a potato.

Rufus shuddered. Even before his eyes could focus, he knew that the big thing was something bad – something to be feared. He could smell evil. It smelt like sweaty fish. Rufus wasn't sure if fish could sweat, but if they did, they would smell just like his bedroom did at that moment. He reached for his bedside lamp and flicked it on.

The room illuminated and Rufus thought he could see a ... no ... it couldn't be ... He blinked as his eyes got used to the light. On his windowsill stood a knobbly, round creature, shorter than a grown-up but much fatter than anybody Rufus had ever seen. It had yellow eyes and green saliva dripped from its chapped lips. On its head were two short, stumpy horns set between short, thick brown hair that appeared to have been cut with shears. It wore no clothes, just a grubby cloth to hide its smelly bottom.

Rufus felt his heart beating rapidly in his chest. The creature looked a bit like the troll from his *Three Billy Goats Gruff* book, but its skin was much less green – it was pink with a faint greenish tinge. In fact, if it weren't for the horns, Rufus might have thought the creature were just an ugly human.

The creature stared back at the little boy, unperturbed at being spotted. "Yummy!" it croaked, licking its lips.

Quickly, Rufus turned the light off and pulled his duvet up to his nose. He peered over the edge, shivering with fear.

Suddenly, he heard an almighty, crackling creak. It sounded like wood splintering as the wind tore branches from a tree. At first, Rufus wondered what was happening, but then he realised that the creature was trying to get its enormous body through the relatively small window into Rufus's bedroom.

For a few moments, Rufus thought he was safe – surely a creature so fat couldn't get through a window so small? – but then there was a loud 'pop' and the creature plopped into the room. It fell, face first, onto the carpet. Then, it brushed itself off and stood up. It glared at Rufus with a hungry glint in its eyes.

Rufus tried to scream but found that he couldn't make a sound. The fear had turned his mouth dry like a cream cracker in the desert. Then, he realised he could bang on the wall –

surely his mum and dad would hear him over their television ...?

However, before Rufus could pull himself up to bang on the wall, the creature hobbled closer and reached out its porky arms. "This is it!" thought Rufus, "I'm going to be eaten by a troll!"

Then, all of a sudden, he heard a high-pitched whistling sound. A long, purple arrow shot in through the window and drove straight into the creature's bottom!

The troll let out an almighty roar, dribbled green slime, and then flopped to the ground.

Rufus watched the monster in disbelief. Was it dead? What had happened? Where had that arrow come from? He edged out of bed and went to the window. However, all he could see was the ordinary Sludgeside street, shrouded in moonlight.

He turned back to face his bedroom and found, to his surprise, that the monster had gone. He couldn't believe it. Quickly, he looked under his bed and in his wardrobe, but there was nothing there apart from dirty socks and pressed clothes. The troll had definitely vanished.

Rufus Sebbleford didn't get a wink of sleep that night. He knew that he'd seen something remarkable. It would be four years before he fully understood what had happened that night – the night when he was five years three-hundred and sixty-four days old.

* * *

It all took place in Sludgeside – a pretty village riddled with rivers and streams, which led to a big, fat, muddy creek. The village was surrounded by hills and overlooked by an ancient, dark and dangerous woodland called the Fusty Forest. Most villagers felt that the greatest threat to their safety were the crocodiles in the deep, treacherous rivers, but that is because they didn't know about the hungry trolls living in the Fusty Forest.

It was late spring during the year that Rufus Sebbleford turned ten. New leaves meant that tree climbers could hide with ease. The lighter evenings allowed children to play outside after dinner. The warm rain made the ground especially squelchy.

Over the four years since his first troll encounter, Rufus had grown taller but no wider. His red hair had darkened slightly and grown thicker, spiking out in every direction. When he smiled, he didn't just smile, he grinned with every inch of his body – his pink lips bared two rows of shiny teeth, his blue eyes twinkled and wrinkled in the corners and he always clenched his fists with excitement. He was one of the most excitable boys in the world, and his teacher considered him something of a handful.

Rufus told his teacher, "When I grow up, I'm going to be a troll hunter!"

The class sniggered.

"That's very brave of you, but a troll hunter isn't a real job," explained Mr Crimplemop.

The teacher was young – only twenty-five, and not considerably tall. He had wild, curly brown hair and a boyish dimple on his left cheek. He wore corduroy trousers and cardigans to try to make him look older, but they didn't. His class liked him a lot.

"It *is* a real job," argued Rufus. "A troll hunter saved my life when I was five."

The class laughed again. Barry Blither's enormous nose snorted like a horn with bogies up it.

Mr Crimplemop looked at Rufus, holding back a little smile. "You have an overactive imagination, Rufus."

"No I haven't ..." he tried to object.

"Polly, what would you like to be when you grow up?" asked Mr Crimplemop, trying to change the subject to something less daft.

"A mad scientist!" announced Polly Chromatic, with a big grin. Her uneven brown pigtails were fixed with green paperclips. Her school uniform swamped her – she wasn't short but had inherited her clothes from her much larger sister. She used multi-coloured elastic bands to keep her trousers and sleeves rolled up.

Mr Crimplemop withheld a smile. Polly was brainy enough to be a scientist and certainly zany. "Well, you'd better work hard then," he told her.

"I'm going to be a princess," offered Anita Grumblenose, without being asked.

"Me too!" sang Aala Snickermouth.

"What are you going to be when you grow up?" Rufus asked the teacher.

"A teacher of a well-behaved class," Mr Crimplemop said with a smile. He decided that the conversation had become far too silly and allowed them to go to break a few minutes early.

As they were leaving the class, somebody grabbed Rufus's arm. He could smell fizzy-strawberry shampoo and bicycle oil, so he knew it must be Polly.

"I believe you," she whispered. "About

trolls, I mean."

"You do?" he asked, turning to face her. Nobody had ever believed him about trolls. Once or twice people had played along, as if it was all a big game, but nobody had truly believed him. "Why?" he asked.

"Because when you talk about them, you look truly scared." She pulled him to the side of the playground. "You've seen one, haven't you?" she enquired, gravely.

Rufus thought about it for a moment. He had tried telling people about the night the troll came in through his window before, but they always said it was a dream. He thought of the troll's yellow eyes and shuddered. "Yes," he whispered.

"What was it like?" asked Polly, eagerly.

"Terrifying," he said, with a gulp. "And very smelly."

"Smelly?"

"It smelt like sweaty fish!"

"Yuck!"

"It was disgusting but also ... kind of ..."

"Kind of what?"

"Kind of stupid," he admitted. "It squashed itself through my window even though it could barely fit. I didn't think about it at the time, because I was only little, but if it had turned sideways, it could have got though much more easily."

"Wait? A troll *climbed in* through your window!" gasped Polly.

"It squeezed in."

"Were you scared?"

"Very!"

Polly shivered.

"But somebody shot it with an arrow and saved me."

"Who?" she asked.

"A troll hunter," explained Rufus. "Must have been."

"Wow!" gasped Polly.

"I know Mr Crimplemop thinks that 'troll hunter' is not a real job, but it must be, mustn't it? I looked and there are no troll hunting classes at college, so I've been teaching myself."

"Really? Wow!"

"Yes, I've built a den at the bottom of my garden. It overlooks the river Muckygush and you can see the Fusty Forest on the other side. It's my lookout post."

"Can I see it?" asked Polly, looking both frightened and thrilled.

Rufus looked at Polly and took a deep breath. She was a nice girl, perhaps a little strange at times, but perfectly pleasant. What's more, she was the first person who had ever taken his troll story seriously. "It's not for the fainthearted," he warned her.

"That's okay, I'm not fainthearted," replied Polly, scooping up a large spider and patting it affectionately on the head.

Chapter 2

The Sheep Chase

Bruno wasn't happy about stealing a sheep from Farmer Fickletrout's field – not happy at all. "Are you sure nobody is coming?" he asked his twin little sisters, for the umpteenth time.

"The coast is clear!" Belinda assured him.

Bruno was a young troll – only ten years old. He looked much like his elders but had honest hazel eyes. Just like the others, his skin was pink with a greenish tinge but it was much less cracked than the older trolls'. His nose was less snotty and his mouth was less slimy. He kept his brown hair short and clean.

His seven-year-old sisters looked similar to Bruno but had long, glossy brown locks and even bigger hazel eyes. They were identical twins but Bruno could always tell them apart from their mannerisms and expressions. Betty was slightly more silly than Belinda.

Bruno took a deep breath, and leapt over the fence. His feet landed in a patch of sticky, squelchy sludge. The warm, spring rain had turned the grass into a mud rink. He ran towards the flock. His actions were met by a chorus of terrified bleating as sheep scurried in every direction. Bruno, equipped with his special sheep-catching gloves, ran after one particularly podgy ewe. After much panting and bleating, a cluster of sheep were trapped in a corner of the field. If there's one thing that's even stupider than a troll, it's a sheep.

Mind you, Bruno and his sisters were smarter than most trolls because their father, Marv the Magnificent, had been the cleverest troll in the land – that was, until he vanished one day without a trace.

Remembering his father made Bruno more determined to catch a sheep for their dinner. Marv would have fed his family, and now it was Bruno's turn. He might only be ten, but he was the man of the family and even in troll culture, that held certain outdated yet powerful expectations. He lunged forward and grabbed the plump sheep. His Velcro gloves attached themselves to the creature's woolly body. The sheep was trapped!

"Hurry up!" cried Betty, suddenly.

"I can see Farmer Fickletrout!" cried Belinda, "And he looks mad!"

"Hide!" shouted Bruno.

"But ..." objected his sisters, in unison.

"Don't worry about me!" ordered Bruno. He watched as the seven-year-olds ran for shelter in the adjacent field. Suddenly, Bruno saw the hunched, fuming shadow of Farmer Fickletrout approaching. He was a rural-looking chap with shaggy, white hair and a stubbly face. He was shaking a hairy fist with rage. In the other hand was a shiny pitchfork.

Bruno realised that he had to get away as quickly as he possibly could. "Abort mission! Abandon sheep!" he told himself. However, when he tried to let go of the sheep, his Velcro gloves remained stuck onto the sheep's woolly coat. "I've got to take off my gloves!" he thought. However, his gloves were a tight fit and simply pulling his arms backwards did not loosen them.

He pulled and he pulled but the sheep came with him! There was no way he could get his left glove off without the help of his right hand. But his right hand was Velcroed to the sheep. There was no way he could get his right glove off without the help of his left hand but his left hand was Velcroed to the sheep. There was only one option – he had to leave the field with the sheep attached!

Farmer Fickletrout entered the field and charged forward. "Let go of my sheep, you vile thief! Let go of my sheep or I'll prong your bottom!" He waved his sharp fork in a threatening manner.

When Bruno saw how upset the farmer was, he wanted more than ever to leave the sheep unharmed, but he couldn't get his gloves off.

"I can't let go of the sheep!" Bruno tried to explain.

"I'll get you!" yelled Farmer Fickletrout.

"Please don't hurt me! If you just help me take these gloves of, then I promise not to steal your sheep!"

"Scoundrel!" bellowed the farmer. "You think you can trick *me*?"

But Bruno *wasn't* trying to trick the farmer. He really was sorry and he really *didn't* want to hurt the sheep, even if it meant his family had to go hungry.

However, the farmer was not going to see reason. He was far too angry. Bruno knew that if he didn't get away quickly, then the farmer really would prong his bottom with the pitchfork. It would be worse than when he sat on a hedgehog.

Bruno tried running, but the sheep couldn't keep up. Its little legs struggled. And so, Bruno raised his arms, lifting the sheep in the air, and charged off as fast as he could.

I doubt you've ever seen a troll carry a sheep, but it is certainly a silly sight.

He ran and he ran, until he got to a wall. He tried to leap onto the wall but it's hard to be springy with a sheep Velcroed to your fingertips. The sheep was too heavy.

Eventually, he managed to pull his bottom up onto the wall. Then, with an almighty heave, he lugged the sheep up next to him.

The farmer was gaining on him rapidly. In his haste, Bruno rolled off the wall onto the road. The sheep, of course, rolled down on top of him. *Thud.*

Farmer Fickletrout reached the wall. He tried to climb onto it but his bones were too creaky. Bruno picked himself up and hurried to the neighbouring field where his little sisters awaited him.

Betty squealed with joy when she saw that Bruno was safe. Belinda smiled to herself; she had always known that her brother could do it. They let 'Bruno plus sheep' in through a wide metal gate.

"Help me get these gloves off!" pleaded Bruno.

"What a tasty sheep!" sang Betty, with glee.

"Lamb chops!" grinned Belinda.

"We're letting him go," Bruno explained.

"Why?" demanded his sisters.

"Please, just help me with these gloves."

Belinda and Betty reluctantly helped their brother take off his gloves.

Bruno gave the sheep a quick pat. "Go on then!" he whispered. The sheep bleated hysterically and ran toward the open gate.

When Farmer Fickletrout saw that his prize sheep was safe and sound, he wept with delight. He wrapped his arms around it and licked it on the nose. *Yuck.*

"Why did you let it go?" asked Belinda, looking disapproving. "That was our dinner!"

"This stops now!" said Bruno. "No more stealing animals. I can't do it anymore."

"But we steal animals so that we don't have to eat human children," Belinda reminded him.

"There must be another way," Bruno told her. "Eating children is wrong, but so is stealing sheep."

"But what other way?" asked Betty.

"I don't know ... yet," admitted Bruno, "but trust me – I will think of something."

Rosen Trevithick

Chapter 3

The Best Den Ever

It was Saturday afternoon. Mr and Mrs Sebbleford were watching a makeover programme on the television called *Horse Versus Poodle*. Rufus was bored out of his mind. So, when Polly rang the doorbell he rushed to answer it. His mum and dad didn't even notice that he'd left the room.

"Hi!" he grinned.

"Hiya!" smiled Polly. She began taking off her rainbow wellies.

"Leave them on," said Rufus. "Let's go 'round the back."

Rufus led Polly along a pebbled path to the back of his house. Polly looked around Rufus's garden in awe. Her family didn't have a garden, just a gravel patch where they kept the wheelie bins.

The Sebbleford family, on the other hand, had a large expanse of lush grass. Blossoming apple trees covered the lawn like clouds of snowflakes waiting to flurry. A tidy wall of conifers framed two sides of the garden and the lower edge was made of boulders that met a deep, dark river – the river Muckygush.

Nearer the water were some prickly bushes and gnarly trees. Polly looked around for Rufus's den.

"You can't see it from here," explained Rufus, as if reading her mind. "It's camouflaged."

"Wow!" exclaimed Polly, with excitement. She hurried down the garden after Rufus.

"I'm glad you're dressed for climbing," he said, looking at Polly's denim dungarees and her colourful wellies.

"Climbing?" repeated Polly. "Why?"

Rufus said nothing and kept walking purposefully toward the bottom of the garden.

They had almost reached the river, but she still couldn't see the den – just thick brambles, ferns and nettles. Then, suddenly, Rufus grabbed what appeared to be a branch, and gave it a tug. Polly quickly realised it was not a branch at all, but a small door woven from sticks and leaves. She was amazed.

Rufus held the door open and beckoned for Polly to go inside. She stepped forwards in awe. What would Rufus's den be like inside?

At first, she couldn't see a thing, because it was dark and gloomy, but then Rufus flicked a switch and an enormous battery-operated torch illuminated the room.

The den was rather spacious – smaller than her bedroom but bigger than a shed. It had a dark red floor made from old carpet tiles, stools made from upturned paint tubs and a little table made from what appeared to be a cable reel.

"Would you like a drink?" offered Rufus.

"There are refreshments?" squeaked Polly. This was the single most exciting place that she'd been to in her life.

"I always keep a bottle of lemonade in here," Rufus told her. "You have to keep your energy up when troll hunting. There's chocolate in my troll hunting kit for the same reason."

"You have a troll hunting kit?"

"Yes."

"What else is in it?"

"A sharp stone, in case I ever get tied up."

"Good idea!"

"A paperclip in case I need to pick a lock."

"Smart."

"And some nose plugs."

"Why do you need those?"

"To block my nostrils – trolls are really stinky."

"Do trolls come into your garden?" asked Polly, suddenly feeling unnerved.

"I don't think so," Rufus told her. "I don't think they can cross the river."

As Rufus poured Polly a plastic cup of lemonade, she continued looking around. It was then that she noticed a ladder in the far corner. It was a funny sort of ladder – a plank with branches nailed to it. "What's up there?" asked Polly.

"Come on," said Rufus, getting up. "I'll show you."

Polly followed Rufus up the ladder. Her heart was pounding with excitement.

When they reached the top, Polly found herself standing on a rickety wooden platform, supported by the branches of an oak tree. It was almost entirely surrounded by a leafy fence. There was a gap at the back, which led to a fireman's pole.

"In case we ever have to make a quick

getaway," explained Rufus, pointing to the pole.

Polly stood up and looked at the deep, dark river. It was the width of an ordinary road and its surface reflected the creepy trees on the far bank. There was a particularly large overhanging tree over there and Polly wished it were on this side so that she could climb it

She looked across the river Muckygush to the Fusty Forest. The woodland was made up of many different kinds of tree – fir, sycamore, oak ... It looked gloomy and creepy. She could only see two rows of trees before their low branches gobbled up the view.

Then, she thought she saw something move in the shadows. She gasped.

"Get down!" whispered Rufus, grabbing the back of her dungarees and tugging her down. They crouched against the wooden floor, concealed behind the fence covered in leaves.

"Are there trolls over there?" asked Polly.

"I think so," Rufus told her. Then he admitted, "I haven't seen one since I was five years, three-hundred and sixty-four days old, but I've seen *evidence*."

"Evidence?" asked Polly, trembling.

"Yes, sometimes in the daylight, I can see troll prints with my binoculars."

"Really?" gasped Polly. "What does a troll print look like?"

"Much like a human footprint, but wider and with one less toe."

"A troll only has four toes!"

"Yes."

"How many fingers does it have?"

"I don't know. Trolls don't walk on their hands so their fingers leave no evidence."

"What about the troll that climbed in through your window?"

"Polly, I thought I was going to be eaten. I didn't have time to count its fingers!"

"Fair point," admitted Polly. "Have you seen any other evidence of trolls?"

"The next thing is scary," Rufus warned her.

"How scary?"

"Very scary!"

"Tell me!"

"I don't know if that's a good idea ..."

"Please!"

Rufus studied Polly. She seemed pretty tough – not the sort of child who was likely to faint or become hysterical. He had once seen her pick up a mangled dead mouse that she found in the playground.

"Okay," agreed Rufus, "but I'm warning

you, it's not nice ..."

"Go on ..." urged Polly, bravely.

"Bones," he whispered, looking grave.

Polly shuddered. "What sort of bones?"

"Children's bones."

Polly gasped.

"At first I thought that the crocodiles were to blame but ..."

"Wait! There are crocodiles in that river?"

"Yes. The Muckygush is one of the most dangerous rivers in the world – deep, fast-flowing and full of crocs!"

Polly grabbed a branch to steady herself.

"Crocodiles can digest bones," explained Rufus. "So something else must be eating the children."

Polly gulped. She was tough, as children go, but crocodiles and child-eating trolls was scary even to her.

"Don't worry," said Rufus, sensing her fear. "The crocodiles can't come into my garden. The bank is too steep on this side. And I don't think trolls can swim, otherwise I would find troll prints on this side of the river."

"But one climbed in your window once, didn't it? It was over this side." Polly reminded him.

Rufus gulped. "Yes, yes it was."

"What are we going to do?" asked Polly. "We can't let them keep eating children, but how are we going to stop them?"

"I don't know yet," admitted Rufus. "I am still studying them. I need to know their strengths, weaknesses, what they watch on telly ..."

"Do trolls watch telly?" asked Polly.

"I don't know yet," Rufus confessed. "But I intend to find out. Then, when I know all about trolls, I will hatch a plan to rid Sludgeside of them all!"

Chapter 4

The Human Pretence Plan

Ma Super-Troll-Knobbly-Foot sat in the corner of the main troll cave. The corner was where she liked to be – away from the other trolls with their smelly bottoms, revolting belches and inexcusable eating habits.

"Join us!" boomed Gunkfreak, one of the largest and most revolting trolls. "We got tasty, plump schoolgirl for supper."

Ma Super-Troll-Knobbly-Foot was disgusted. How could her fellow trolls think it was acceptable to eat schoolchildren? She was a thoroughbred troll and yet she could see that it was wrong, so why couldn't they?

Her stomach gurgled. She was very hungry, but she just couldn't bring herself to eat a human. Her troll children would be home soon with supper for the family, probably roast lamb. Ma didn't like having to ask her children to hunt for her but ever since she injured her leg in an unfortunate hula hooping accident, she had been unable to move quickly. As for her good-for-nothing husband, he had disappeared without a trace many years before. She still hadn't forgiven him.

She felt a breeze and looked up. Somebody had shifted the stone that sealed the entrance to the sprawling cave network where sixteen and a half trolls nested. In walked her son, Bruno, followed by her two daughters, Belinda and Betty.

Ma Super-Troll-Knobbly-Foot breathed a sigh of relief. Hunting for farm animals was dangerous and she always feared for their lives whenever her children went out in search of dinner. She wondered what they had caught today. However, as they grew closer, she saw that her children's arms were empty.

"Where be dinner?" she asked. As with most trolls, her English wasn't very good.

"I couldn't do it," explained Bruno, whose English was somewhat better due to the intelligence he'd inherited from his brainy father.

"Couldn't do it?" echoed Ma.

"The farmer cried," explained Betty.

Ma looked unimpressed.

"The farmer was very upset," Bruno told her. Then, he added, "Stealing animals ,is wrong."

Suddenly, he heard a roar of laughter. He turned and saw Gunkfreak and the others rolling around, laughing their socks off (or they would have been, if trolls wore socks.)

"It's true!" insisted Bruno. "I know the sheep are farmed to be eaten, but they're not *ours*. They belong to Farmer Fickletrout."

Gunkfreak bellowed with laughter. "Pathetic!"

Ma put an arm around Bruno and guided him further into the corner of the cave, making sure that the twins were following.

"Eat sheep – save humans," she reminded her son.

"I know," he agreed. "And it's better to steal animals from fields than children from their beds, but I don't want to do *either*."

Ma churned the information around in her mind. Her mind worked very slowly, so it took some time. She knew it wasn't right to steal sheep, but if they didn't steal sheep then what would they eat? She couldn't have her family go hungry. A troll can't live on vegetables alone.

Being a single mother can be tough for anybody, but it's especially hard for a troll. It isn't like being a human. A human single mother can look for a job to earn money for food. If she doesn't find one then her government will help with food money until she does.

It was then that Ma Super-Troll-Knobbly-Foot had a brainwave – perhaps the only brainwave of her life. "Pretend humans!" she cried.

"What?" asked her three children, together.

"Humans be getting food with money. No hunt," she explained.

"But they have to have jobs to get the money," Bruno reminded her. He didn't want to offend his mother, but she could hardly walk since the unfortunate hula hooping accident and she wasn't very smart. He didn't think she would find it easy to get a job.

"Benefits," she grunted.

"What's she talking about?" asked Betty.

"Humans have taxes," explained Bruno. "People with jobs give money to the government and then the government gives some of it to people who are less fortunate, to stop them from starving."

"So, if we pretend to be human, we'll be given help, and we won't have to steal sheep anymore!" Betty cried, sounding excited.

"Wait!" interrupted Belinda, the voice of reason. "How are we going to convince anybody that we're human? Our skin has a greenish tinge, we're much podgier than humans, our saliva is green, and then there's *these*!" She pointed to the short, dumpy horns on her forehead.

"I didn't say it be easy!" replied Ma.

"Hats!" cried Betty. "We'll wears hats to cover our horns!"

"Fake tan!" added Bruno. "I've seen humans use it! It makes you orange and would easily cover up our skin's greenish tinge."

"Bubble gum!" Betty suggested. "We will chew coloured bubble gum and tell people that that's why our spit is not clear."

"Chocolate fingers!" shouted Ma.

They all looked at her.

"How will chocolate fingers help, Ma?" asked Bruno.

"They won't," admitted Ma. "I just like chocolate fingers."

Bruno laughed. "Are we really going to try this?" he asked.

"Yarb!" replied Ma, which is troll for 'yes'.

"So, we'll disguise ourselves as humans and live in a house." He looked around at the cave and the smelly trolls in it; he felt he would much prefer to live in a house. "We'll get money from the government for food. And … oh narb!" cried Bruno.

"What?" asked the others.

"We won't have to go to school, will we?"

Chapter 5

The Peculiar New Boy

Two weeks later, Rufus Sebbleford was hurrying to school. He had exciting news for Polly. It didn't take him long to find her. She stood out because she was wearing her brown hair in a high ponytail fixed with clothes pegs.

"Good morning, Polly," he said with a grin.

"Sebbleford!" yelled Barry Blithers. "Why are you talking to a girl?" He looked as if his eyes might pop out of his plump, rosy face. He had thin black hair, an upturned nose that resembled a snout, and tiny grey eyes. Barry was a thug – the meanest boy in the school. But Rufus wasn't scared of Barry.

"Oh get lost, Blithers!" replied Rufus. He didn't care what other children thought. Polly believed in real trolls and that was all that mattered.

"Morning, Rufus," called Polly, with a big grin.

The other girls looked around and stared. "Do you have a new boyfriend?" drawled Anita Grumblenose, sniggering. She was a pretty girl with blonde hair and blue eyes but her beauty was only skin-deep. She was like an ornate jar of wriggling maggots.

Aala Snickermouth looked at Rufus and giggled nastily. Equally pretty, she was also almost as annoying. She was friendly on her own but not when Anita was around. Aala's grandfather was from Turkey and she'd inherited her family's dark, shiny hair and smooth, brown skin. She was like an ornate jar of fruit in which a few maggots, escaped from Anita, wriggled.

Polly didn't care for the other girls in her class. She had had more fun climbing trees with Rufus during one afternoon than she had ever had reciting boring skipping songs with Anita and Aala. The girls could think what they liked.

"I've got something to tell you!" Rufus began. "In private. Come on ..." he led Polly away to the corner of the yard. Polly was intrigued. What could Rufus be waiting to tell her?

"Are you going kissing?" giggled Anita.

Rufus and Polly ignored her.

"What is it?" asked Polly.

"I saw one!" he told her.

"A troll?" cried Polly.

"Yes!" he said.

"In the forest?" she asked.

"No, it was on the way to school. I was just crossing the bumpy bridge over the stream by the crooked church and I smelt something disgusting like a rotten egg with a sprout festering inside. I peered under the bridge and then I saw the troll. It tried to press itself against the wall so that I couldn't see it but it was fat and round like a giant potato. There was no mistaking it."

"Were you scared?" asked Polly.

"No," admitted Rufus, bravely. "Funnily enough, I wasn't scared. *It* seemed to be hiding from *me*."

"Why would it do that?"

"I don't know. Perhaps because it's daylight and there are lots of people around. If the masses found out about real trolls they would hunt them down."

Suddenly, they heard a crash. They turned

to face the source of the clatter and were surprised by what they saw. A very fat woman had walked straight into the school gate! The gate fell off its hinges and crashed down onto the playground. Everybody turned and stared as the lady hobbled in.

The fat woman was very peculiar looking. She was little more than a metre tall. Her skin was bright orange, like somebody who had been in the sun for far too long. The features on her face were large – she had a wide nose, thick lips and chubby cheeks. Her clothes looked as though they had been made from rubbish. Her dress appeared to have been made from a white pillowcase and she wore a tinfoil necklace. On her head was the weirdest hat that any of the children had ever seen – it was made from an upturned pudding basin covered in paper flowers. On her feet – flippers!

When she stepped into the playground, Rufus and Polly could see three smaller people behind her. They were the oddest children that anybody had ever seen. They were all enormously wide, they were all orange and they all wore bizarre hats.

The biggest of the children was wearing a school uniform made of paper. He had a round, white hat like a sailor. The smaller two were wearing school dresses made from painted newspaper and had tea cosies on their heads. Each 'girl' had four untidy pigtails poking out from beneath their unusual headgear.

"Who are they?" whispered Polly.

"I don't know," replied Rufus. "But it looks as though they are coming to our school."

"Good afternoon!" sang the lady, proudly.

"Ma," whispered the boy. "It's morning."

"Morning afternoon!" sang the lady.

The boy face-palmed.

"Where be the head teacher?" she demanded.

On hearing the commotion, Mr Grubstopper hurried out of his office and into the playground. He was a tidy little man with grey hair and perfectly round glasses. He wore expertly pressed shirts, which he replaced whenever he ripped a stitch. Today's shirt looked whiter than white as if it were bathed in ultra-violet light. "I am the head teacher," he explained. "How may I help you?"

"Me children school!" boomed the woman.

"What she means," interrupted the little boy, "is that my sisters and I would like to join Sludgeside School."

Anita and her cronies started giggling. "Look at their clothes! Perhaps they should join *play*school."

"I am ten," said the boy, "and my sisters are seven." They looked a little short for their ages but then some children grow faster than others.

"You can't just turn up at my school and expect to join. There is a process!" barked Mr Grubstopper.

The woman looked blank.

"There are forms!" explained the head, exasperated.

"We just want to learn," explained the boy. The newspaper-clad girls nodded enthusiastically.

"Which school did you come from?" asked the head teacher.

"Um ..." thought the boy.

"Um ..." echoed the girls.

"Er ..." mumbled the woman.

"I need records from your previous school," explained the head teacher. "Why don't you go away and fill in the forms. Then I'll look up your records and ..."

Crunch!

Everybody looked around. One of the twins had walked into a flowerbed. Everybody watched as she plucked a dahlia and then started to poke the stalk up her nose. Polly rushed forward and seized the flower. "You mustn't put flowers up your nose," she explained, kindly.

The head teacher looked shocked.

"My sisters need an education," explained the peculiar-looking boy. "What does it matter where we came from or whether or not we've filled in the forms? We need to be taught, and you're here to teach. Now what do you say?"

Mr Grubstopper looked at the other twin, who was attempting to put mud in her ears. There was no doubt that these children needed a good school.

Mr Grubstopper looked at the boy.

The boy's wide hazel eyes gazed back.

"Oh, all right," he said, taking a deep breath. "But those uniforms will not do."

"Thank you!" cried the boy. He was so happy that he kissed the head teacher! This left purple, bubble-gum flavoured slime on the teacher's cheek.

Mr Grubstopper stumbled backwards with shock. He took an antibacterial tissue from his pocket and wiped his face.

When, finally, he had managed to steady himself, he asked, "What are your names?"

"I'm Bruno," explained the boy. "And these are my twin little sisters, Betty and Belinda."

Mr Grubstopper looked at the woman.

"And that's Ma," Bruno told him.

"Ma what?" asked the head.

"Ma Super ..." but then Bruno remembered that using their long name, 'Super-Troll-Knobbly-Foot', would give the game away. So instead, he opted for something short, "Ma Trolly," he said. Then, he realised that 'trolly' could mean 'like a troll', which was far too obvious. So he added, "I mean, Trolley – like a shopping trolley."

"Welcome to the school then, Trolley family," said Mr Grubstopper. "However, we don't allow hats in this school. You will have to remove them, I'm afraid."

The trolls grabbed their headwear and held them firmly against their heads. They couldn't take them off because the horns that lay beneath would show people that the Trolleys were not really a human family.

"Hats on!" boomed Ma.

"We never take our hats off," Bruno told him. Luckily his eyes fell on Aala, who was wearing a hijab. "That girl is wearing a scarf on her head."

"That's different. Miss Snickermouth wears a hijab for religious reasons."

"We religious!" barked Ma.

"Yarb, that's right!" fibbed Bruno. "I mean *yes,* that's right. We are a very religious family. We wear hats for religious reasons too."

Mr Grubstopper looked at the pudding basin, the sailor hat and the tea cosies with suspicion. "What religion?" he asked.

Bruno looked around the playground for inspiration. Eventually his eyes fell on the hopscotch court. "Hopscotchism!" he said, thinking on his feet.

The head teacher's eyes widened. "Hopscotchism?" he repeated. "Never heard of it."

Ma tried her hardest to look offended. Betty pretended to cry.

The last thing Mr Grubstopper wanted to seem was intolerant of other people's religions. So, despite being an educated man, he said, "Hopscotchism, indeed. Now I think about it, I do remember Hopscotchism. In fact, I know it well. I went to a Hopscotch service just last week. Good for you. We do pride ourselves on being diverse here at Sludgeside School. Welcome Bruno, Betty and Belinda. You may, of course, keep your ... er ... hats on."

Bruno winked at his sisters. They had done it! They had duped the head teacher and got in to Sludgeside School. None of them really wanted to do lessons, but now that they belonged to a school, they were one step closer to living like humans. If they succeeded in their mission, they would be able to satisfy their appetites without ever having to steal another farm animal or eat a human child. Bruno looked at the happy, healthy, non-nibbled children around him and felt sure that they were doing the right thing.

Chapter 6

A Lesson in Bendy Mirrors

Mr Crimplemop stood at the front of his class, surveying the destruction already caused by his new pupil. There was paint on the floor from when Bruno walked into an easel. Most of the children glimmered in the light because Bruno had shaken glitter over them, thinking it was a flying potion. And now the class hamster was running loose, because Bruno had left the hatch of the cage open thinking it would help it to breathe. Chaos, glitter and runaway rodents – what on earth was wrong with the new boy?

Bruno may have been clever for a troll, but having got to age ten without going to school, he was nowhere near as smart as a ten-year-old human. He was not just uneducated but incredibly disruptive. Of course, Mr Crimplemop had no idea that Bruno was a troll, or indeed, that trolls really existed. So instead of understanding Bruno's behaviour, he thought he was just very naughty.

"What do you think of the new boy?" Polly asked Rufus.

"He's lively, isn't he?" Rufus replied.

"Yes! He certainly is. He seems friendly though."

"That's true," agreed Rufus. "I wonder why he's so orange."

"Perhaps he's from another country."

"What country has orange people?"

"I don't know. Whichever country has Hopscotchism, I suppose."

"I've never heard of Hopscotchism."

"Me neither." Polly looked thoughtful.

"What are you thinking?" asked Rufus.

"Something about the new family isn't quite right. I just don't know what it is."

Mr Crimplemop wondered if it was the right time to deliver his bendy mirrors lesson. Usually he loved teaching his class about bendy mirrors because they always really enjoyed it. However, it usually made the children excitable and today, they were already more excitable than a Jack Russell on Smarties.

He glanced over at the new boy, who was sitting on his desk trying to balance a mouse-shaped rubber on his bulbous nose.

"What have I told you about chairs?" he asked Bruno.

"Oops! Sorry," responded Bruno, looking genuinely apologetic. "They're for sitting on. Right. Got it this time."

It had only been three minutes since Mr Crimplemop had first taught Bruno about chairs. This boy's memory seemed even shorter than a goldfish's memory.

The other children giggled as Bruno plopped into his chair, accidentally doing a bottom burp as his bum collided with the wooden surface.

Mr Crimplemop sighed. Perhaps it would be a good idea to have a quiet afternoon reading books and writing answers to questions.

"When are you going to teach us about bendy mirrors?" asked Rufus.

"Drat!" thought Mr Crimplemop. He had forgotten that he'd already promised them the science lesson. "All right," he said, with a reluctant sigh. "Get into groups of three." The teacher looked at his empty Mr Splendiferous Science Park mug, and begun counting down the minutes until he could get a refill. The zany chap who ran the science park (Mr Splendiferous) was none other than Mr Crimplemop's uncle. He had given him that mug for his birthday and the teacher's cups of tea helped him get through days like this. Mr Crimplemop hadn't yet told his class that he was related to Mr Splendiferous because he was planning to surprise them one day.

Polly leant over and whispered to Rufus. "Can we ask Bruno to join us?"

Rufus looked at Bruno, who was trying to swallow a ruler. "I'm not sure ..." he stuttered.

Bruno got out of his chair and took a step towards a table of pretty girls. "Don't come any closer!" Anita ordered. Then she added, nastily, "I can smell you from here!"

Aala and Barry snorted with laughter.

The poor new boy was clearly upset. Rufus felt sorry for him. Admittedly, Bruno was not the most fragrant of his classmates, but he didn't deserve to be embarrassed like that.

"Come and join *us*!" Rufus invited.

Bruno gave an enormous grin. His cheeks seemed to stretch outwards to accommodate a six-inch smile. Rufus wondered if that ruler was still in there.

"Thank you!" Polly whispered to Rufus,

and moved over to make space for the new boy.

Mr Crimplemop noticed, with dismay, that Bruno had teamed up with Rufus and Polly. They were nice children but they were not exactly 'calm'. He wondered if he should insist that Bruno worked with some quieter people. But, as he watched the three laughing and joking together, he knew it was too late to separate them.

"Right," he told the class. "I need one person from each group to come up and get a set of mirrors and a packet of plasticine."

Before the trio could discuss it, Bruno leapt forward and grabbed a box of mirrors with his teeth.

"Hands please, Bruno!" shouted the teacher.

"Look! It's not even house trained," sniggered Anita.

Polly shot her a furious glare.

Bruno jumped up on the table and opened his mouth, letting the box of mirrors drop. Fortunately, Polly managed to reach out and catch them before they could crash into the table and shatter into tiny pieces.

"These mirrors," explained Mr Crimplemop, "are just like the giant mirrors you will see at a fairground or the science park, except much smaller. So you will need to make yourself a little plasticine figure."

Bruno's hands were already covered in plasticine. He mixed pink, white and a tiny bit of green, until he made a colour that was like human flesh but with a slight greenish tinge – troll colour. Then, using the mixture he had just made, he moulded two spheres. He put the smaller of the two balls on top of the larger, and used the rest of the clay to make arms and legs. Then, he grabbed some white, and started making horns.

Rufus and Polly watched with amazement. Bruno looked up and thought that his new friends were impressed with his modelling skills. He beamed at them. He continued sculpting his plasticine figure. Then, with horror – he realised his mistake – he was making a troll!

Suddenly, he squished the figure into a lump and grabbed some pink. He was supposed to be a human! – that meant making *human* plasticine figures.

Rufus and Polly exchanged excited looks. The new boy knew about trolls too! Until last week, Rufus had thought that he was the only boy in the world who had seen a real troll, and now, right here in front of him, was a boy who knew trolls well enough to sculpt one! Rufus wondered how Bruno could possibly have seen a troll and survived to tell the tale. Of course, he had no way of knowing that the new boy *was* a troll.

Polly studied the new boy with interest. It was then that she noticed something else unusual. "Is that bubble gum in your mouth?" she asked.

"Yes," admitted Bruno who, as you know, had to chew coloured gum to disguise his green troll spit.

"If you get caught chewing that in class, you will be in a lot of trouble," she warned him.

"Religious reasons," fibbed Bruno, quickly. "It's a Hopscotch tradition."

Rufus and Polly exchanged puzzled glances. Rufus wondered if he should ask Bruno about trolls there and then. However, at that moment Mr Crimplemop interrupted.

"I want you to find the mirror that makes your model look taller," he told them. "You will have to bend down to the level of the table to see from the perfect angle."

Bruno held out the plasticine human that he'd just made. It was a schoolgirl with baggy clothes and brown hair in a high ponytail. Polly took the miniature version of herself and placed it in front of the first mirror. It made the model look short and fat. Rufus grabbed the next mirror. Sure enough, the second mirror made the little figure look twice as tall as it really was.

"Found it!" called out Rufus.

The teacher told the class, "Now, look at the back of the mirror and you'll see its description. I want you to write down the words on the back of each mirror next to a drawing of the reflection."

"I don't understand," said Barry Blither.

"What does it say on the back of the mirror that makes your figure tall?" asked Mr Crimplemop.

"Horizontal concave," chorused the class.

"Right, so I want you to write 'horizontal concave' and then draw a tall version of your figure, just as it looks in the mirror."

"Ooh! This is going to be fun!" giggled Rufus, drawing a tall version of the Polly figure that Bruno had made.

"Oi!" laughed Polly, as Rufus dotted the page. "I don't have freckles!"

"Yes, you do!" laughed Rufus.

Polly turned to Bruno. "I don't have freckles, do I?"

"One or two," he admitted. Then, seeing

that she looked hurt, he added "But they are very cute."

Polly blushed, then smiled and started adding freckles to her own illustration.

Rufus realised that if Bruno hadn't squashed his original figure, they would be drawing trolls in their exercise books. Rufus welcomed any opportunity to draw or write about trolls.

He wondered if there was still a troll under the bumpy bridge by the crooked church. He wondered if he should take Polly or his new friend along with him to check after school. However, as he watched them switching mirrors and laughing at reflections, he realised how happy they were. Troll hunting was a serious business. Perhaps it would not be fair to inflict something so horrid on them when they were having such a lovely day.

Bruno was a surprisingly good artist. His pictures of the plasticine figure were so good that they looked like illustrations from a book. Sadly, his grasp of numbers was not as good. He managed to draw a number one, but instead of a two, he drew a snail, and instead of a three, he drew a crab. Polly helped him with his numbers.

In the meantime, Rufus had other things

on his mind – would he see a troll on his way home from school?

* * *

Rufus waited until everybody else had left, before leaving the school grounds. He remembered that troll pressing itself against the wall that morning – it hadn't wanted to be seen. Giggling children and gossiping parents would alert the troll to the fact that there were people around and it would surely hide. Whereas if Rufus sneaked up quietly on his own, he might be able to take the troll by surprise.

This was, of course, purely a surveillance mission. Rufus didn't plan to hurt the troll or capture it. He didn't have his bow and arrow with him, for a start. No, today was about observation. Had he accurately remembered the troll from all those years ago? What could he glean now that he hadn't noticed that night?

This morning, he hadn't been able to ascertain much at all – the troll had moved into the shadows too quickly. If it weren't for its horns, its round, potato-like figure, and of course, Rufus's expertise, he would not have known it was a troll at all.

When finally, the last group of parents left

the playground, Rufus followed them out.

"You're late today," observed Mr Grubstopper, picking bits of fluff off his sleeve. "You usually can't wait to get away."

"I'm tired," lied Rufus, and hurried away.

In his excitement, he walked too quickly. He soon found that he had to slow his pace or he would catch up with the noisy group of parents just ahead of him. His heart pounded in his chest. He could hardly wait to get to the bridge, but he had to be patient. He sniffed the air around him. He could smell cherry blossom and freshly cut grass. But could he also detect eau de troll?

As he neared the bridge, he thought that he could detect the repulsive, sprouty-egg scent of troll. When he reached the edge of the bridge, he crept along the bank and bent down to look beneath.

To his utter disappointment, there was nothing beneath the bridge except a few sticks and a broken bottle. He was bitterly disappointed. He had set his heart on a genuine troll sighting.

How much longer before he could begin following his destiny and become a real troll hunter? How much longer before he could realise his life's ambition? How much longer before he could finally start protecting Sludgeside from the monsters that only he, Polly and Bruno, knew existed? Angrily, he stamped his foot. He huffed, loudly.

However, as he breathed in, he was certain that he caught a whiff of Brussels sprouts. He sniffed again – yes, the pong was undeniable! He looked upstream towards a thick row of trees. Was there something stinky hiding in the shadows?

Without stopping to consider the inevitable danger, Rufus found himself hurrying up the grass verge towards the Fusty Forest. There was a troll up there – he knew it!

He hurried past the first tree, looking around. He couldn't see anything except a broken scooter and a damp, slug-covered armchair. He carried on to the next tree – nothing but a slippery banana skin and a mouldy carrot. He continued. The undergrowth thickened.

Then, he heard something move, just ahead of him. Was it a bird? Was it a rabbit? Was it a ...?

Suddenly, Rufus felt overpowered by an almighty stench. He felt something sting his chest and his body fell backwards. He looked down and realised that somebody had slung a rope around him. Somebody had captured Rufus Sebbleford. That somebody was a troll.

Chapter 7

Gunkfreak's Really Stupid Plan

Bruno looked at the chest of drawers in his new bedroom. He knew that some of his toys were in there, but had no idea how to get to them. He had seen Mr Crimplemop press an eject button to get a shiny disk out of some sort of black box, so he tried pushing the top-drawer knob. Nothing happened. He knew how to push a handle to open a door. He tried pushing down on the top-drawer knob. Nothing happened. Eventually, he pulled the knob. He pulled it so hard that the drawer shot out of the chest, and landed on top of Bruno, on the floor!

Fortunately, Bruno's layers of troll fat protected him from both the fall and the drawer landing on top of him. The drawer bounced off his belly and onto the floor, showering toys everywhere.

Although he was slightly bruised and somewhat stunned, Bruno was delighted to be finally able to get to the contents of the drawer. Eagerly, he looked around. However, no matter how hard he searched, he just couldn't find his boomerang.

He picked himself up and pulled the knob on the second drawer, this time, much more carefully. The drawer opened at a sensible speed and this one did not fall out.

Still, Bruno could not find his boomerang. In fact, he hadn't seen it since they left the cave. He certainly couldn't remember packing it.

Then he remembered why he hadn't seen his boomerang when he was packing. Bruno had found Betty playing with it and, through concern that she might accidentally hit herself in the face, had hidden it on a high ledge out of her reach. A wooden object that returned when thrown was not safe in the hands of a seven-year-old troll.

Bruno felt sad. His boomerang was his favourite possession. It was one of the few things he owned that had neither been stolen nor found in a wheelie bin. Bruno's boomerang was one of a kind. It had a sausage carved into one side and a hippopotamus on the other. It had belonged to his father, Marv the Magnificent. He knew that if his father returned, he would want to know that his boomerang had been well looked after.

Ma had told Bruno not to get his hopes up about this – his father would never return. However, Bruno thought otherwise. He felt that his father was too caring and too responsible to just desert them. He also felt that his father was too smart, too brave and too strong to have come to any harm. There must be a good reason for his disappearance.

Bruno knew he had to get that boomerang back. His mother had expressly forbidden returning to the cave. "If we're going to live like humans, then there is no going back," she had told them. But when Bruno had agreed not to go back to the cave, he had had no idea that his boomerang was still inside!

He crept downstairs. Ma was in the kitchen trying to work out why the refrigerator wasn't cooking her popcorn soup. Bruno suspected it was a puzzle that would keep her busy for quite some time. Quietly, he opened the back door and sneaked out.

* * *

Gunkfreak looked at his catch. The red-haired boy squirming in his net was fairly tall but very bony. He probably wouldn't be able to get much meat off him. Still, the fat, ugly troll had other things on his mind. He would bring the boy back to the cave as a light snack while he told the other trolls about his master plan.

"Let go of me," cried Rufus, kicking his feet as he tried to wriggle free.

Gunkfreak ignored him, and strode forward with Rufus in the net slung over his shoulder.

"I know a troll hunter!" Rufus shouted. "A troll hunter with a bow and arrow! He saved me once before and he'll save me again."

The troll chuckled – a deep, rumbling belly laugh.

"My friend Polly knows all about you! There will be people looking for me!" Rufus told him.

Gunkfreak wasn't scared of Polly, whoever she might be. He wasn't scared of Rufus. And he certainly wasn't scared of the mystery archer. He marched up the stream towards the troll cave. Gunkfreak had always suspected that he was the best troll. When he told the others about his plan, they would *know* that he was the best.

They arrived at the Fusty Forest. It was the same dark, sprawling woodland that stretched from the river at the foot of the Sebbleford's garden.

The captive noticed a four-toed troll print on the ground below. As the troll strode forward, Rufus noticed more and more prints. They must be getting near the trolls' lair.

Rufus kept his eyes open the whole way, looking for landmarks so that he could remember the route. That way, when he escaped, he would be able to hurry straight back to the bumpy bridge without risking getting lost in the Fusty Forest. That was *if* he escaped.

The young boy tried to be brave, but this troll was enormous – much larger than the one he'd seen when he was five years, three-hundred and sixty-four days old. And the net was made of thick rope so Rufus stood no chance of breaking it with his hands.

Then, he remembered the troll hunting kit that he kept in his pocket. You don't spend many years dreaming of being a troll hunter without being prepared for troll-on-boy conflict. He tried to move his left arm but it was tangled in the net. He tried to move his right arm, and fortunately, it was just free enough for him to reach into his left pocket and search for the stone.

The troll plunged into the darkest depths of the forest with Rufus slung over his shoulder. He was completely unaware that the little boy was locating his weapon ready for escape.

However, just as Rufus managed to grab the stone, Gunkfreak arrived at the hillside. He stopped walking and, with an almighty shove, dislodged a giant boulder. The boulder sealed the entrance to a cave hidden in the hillside. Gunkfreak marched inside and dropped the net containing Rufus onto the floor of the cave.

Rufus watched with dismay as the troll tugged the boulder back into place. Even if Rufus could cut the net with his stone, he was far too small to move that boulder by himself. Rufus Sebbleford was well and truly trapped.

The worst part was the stench. The troll cave smelt not just like boiled sprouts, but also of steaming poo, runny bogies and slimy, stinky cheese. A weaker boy might have been sick, but not Rufus – he was prepared. He grabbed the nose plugs from his pocket, and promptly shoved them in place. *Much better.*

They appeared to be alone in the cave. The embers of a small fire smouldered near the entrance. Little lanterns framed the area. Rufus could just make out tunnels leading further into the hillside. He wondered what they led to.

"Come!" bellowed Gunkfreak.

Rufus felt the ground rumble. He was confused. Was this a hill or a volcano? But then the source of the rumbling became clear. Big, heavy trolls waddled in from every direction. They were all very similar to Gunkfreak – pink with a greenish tinge, fat, round and with stubby horns. Most wore grubby cloths wrapped around their bottoms. The rest wore what appeared to be pillowcases, bursting at the seams. Some had longer hair than others ranging from mousy to black. Gunkfreak's poo-coloured mop was particularly wild.

Terrified, Rufus began working at the net with his stone. He might not be able to escape through the entrance but perhaps, if he were particularly speedy, he might be able to escape into one of those tunnels.

"A skinny boy?" asked a troll who had a snotty moustache. "Gunkfreak be waking me for a skinny boy?"

"Not just one skinny boy!" boomed Gunkfreak. "One hundred children!"

"One hundred children?"

"I found a box of children!" revealed Gunkfreak.

"A box of children?" asked the others in disbelief.

"Yarb. There be a box made of bricks, and in it be lots of children!"

"You mean a school!" cried a voice.

"Yarb! A school!" agreed Gunkfreak.

This was met by excited muttering. Rufus's heart almost stopped beating. A school? *His* school? What could the troll want with his school?

"But children be going to school in the daytime!" pointed out a troll with three rolls of fat around its waist.

"And we be hunting at night!" cried another voice.

"I got solution!" Gunkfreak announced, proudly. Then, he asked, "What be making it dark – besides night?"

"Black paint?"

"Fire going out?"

"Closing our eyes?"

"You be right!" shouted Gunkfreak, with glee. "Closing our eyes be making it dark. We is going to attack the school with our eyes closed!"

The plan was the stupidest plan that Rufus had ever heard. Yet the trolls responded with complete admiration. Rufus thought that he even heard one of them mutter, "Wowsers." They began talking excitedly among themselves about the number of children they would get to devour.

Rufus felt sick. Of course, he knew that his fellow pupils had nothing to fear from trolls walking around in broad daylight with their eyes closed. But what if one of them came up with a plan that might actually work? Now that his school was a target, there was no telling what the trolls might do. They were undeniably stupid but they were also strong, nasty and there appeared to be quite a few of them. Rufus could count at least ten from where he was.

By now, Rufus had managed to cut a hole the size of a football in the net. He was a skinny boy but his shoulders were wider than a football. Only two or three more cuts and he would be free. He looked around at the circle of trolls surrounding him. There weren't many gaps between them, but there were some. If he took them by surprise then he might be able to hurry through a gap and dash away into one of the tunnels.

Suddenly, the trolls stopped their

enthusiastic chattering as a dark shadow was cast over the cave. Rufus looked up and saw that all of the trolls were looking in the direction of the widest tunnel.

"It's him!" squeaked one.

"The Ogre of Uggle!" whispered another.

But who was The Ogre of Uggle? Rufus had a feeling that he was just about to find out. Even with nose plugs up his nose, he could smell the revolting stench of cabbages rotting in stinky cheese sauce. Whoever The Ogre of Uggle was, he was very, very smelly.

Eventually the troll entered the cave. *Yikes*. The Ogre of Uggle was easily the biggest troll of all. He was twice the size of Gunkfreak, and Gunkfreak was no mouse. Rufus wondered if The Ogre of Uggle were half-giant. The Ogre wore three items of clothing: a grubby white top hat, a ripped orange bow tie, and a pair of enormous yellow y-fronts.

"What be going on?" The Ogre demanded.

"It's Gunkfreak!" cried the moustached troll. "He be having a brain wave!"

"A brainwave?" asked The Ogre, in disbelief. "Do be telling ...?"

Rufus looked at his slimy captor and felt that the name 'Gunkfreak' suited him well. He was trembling. It was odd that the troll who had just been commanding the room had now been reduced to a shivering wreck.

"Um ... yarb," stuttered Gunkfreak.

"Well?"

"We go to a school in the daytime, when it is full of children. Then, we be gobbling them all up!"

"Fool!" cried The Ogre, shaking his gigantic fist.

Gunkfreak trembled.

"We hunt at night!" shouted The Ogre.

"But Gunkfreak has a plan," another troll pointed out. "A plan to make it night ..."

"Make it night?" laughed The Ogre. "And how be you making it night?"

Gunkfreak gulped. "We close our eyes," he mumbled.

"Close our eyes?" boomed The Ogre. "*Close our eyes?*" He began shaking his fist. "That be your idea? Closing our *eyes*?"

"W–what's wrong with that?" stuttered Gunkfreak.

"The reason we be hunting at night, is not so that we can't see *them*. It's so they can't see *us*!" The Ogre pointed out, at extreme volume.

The trolls responded with a chorus of "Oh!" Then they fell about laughing. Gunkfreak's face turned the colour of mouldy beetroot.

Rufus saw his opportunity. Having at last cut a large enough hole, he freed himself from the net. He leapt up and darted towards one of the tunnels that led into the hills.

At first, the trolls were too busy laughing at Gunkfreak to move. But suddenly the snotty, hairy-lipped troll shouted, "Boy! Boy on the loose!"

Fortunately, Rufus was a fast runner and had already made significant headway when the troll spotted him. Once again he heard that sound – like a volcano erupting. The trolls scrambled forward. Rufus dived into the smallest tunnel he could find. He was a skinny boy and if there was one thing a troll is not, it's skinny.

Gunkfreak, trying to redeem himself after his embarrassment, attempted to follow Rufus into the tunnel. However, he was far too fat. It was like a pig trying to squeeze through a letterbox. He got well and truly stuck.

Because Gunkfreak was stuck in the entrance to the tunnel, no other troll could get through, allowing Rufus plenty of time to get away.

The moustached troll grabbed Gunkfreak's sausage legs and began to pull, but his podgy body was still lodged in the tunnel. The troll with three rolls of fat on its waist grabbed the moustached troll, and they both began to pull, but still they could not move Gunkfreak. Finally, The Ogre of Uggle grabbed the fat-rolls troll, who was holding the hairy-lipped troll and they all pulled Gunkfreak's legs.

There was a loud pop, and Gunkfreak was freed from the tunnel. He landed on the moustached troll, who landed on the fat-rolls troll, who landed on The Ogre of Uggle.

From beneath a pile of heavy trolls, The Ogre found it hard to fill his lungs. He wanted to bellow but instead his voice came out soft and squeaky. "Go after him!" he peeped.

The smallest troll, a nasty young monster called Gobb Podgeleton, hurried down the tunnel. He had long, matted hair, angry eyes and sharp teeth.

Gobb hurried into the tunnel wondering whether he'd get to eat all of the boy if he were the one to catch him.

Rufus, who was already some distance ahead, smelt Gobb coming – he smelt like a potty filled with sticky snot. However, he felt sure that he could outrun him. Sure that was, until he met a dead end.

"No!" cried Rufus, as he ran straight into a

rock, grazing his knuckles. Gobb approached, green saliva dripping down his chin like bogies that had lost their way.

Poor Rufus had nowhere to go. Ahead – rock. To the left – rock. To the right – rock. Behind – hungry troll. Rufus closed his eyes and feared the worst.

Then, suddenly, there was a thud. Rufus opened his eyes. The troll before him lay unconscious on the floor. Instinctively, Rufus looked for an arrow. But there was no arrow. Instead, he saw a different object on the ground next to the troll. He picked it up and examined it. It was flat and wooden with a sausage carved into one side and a hippopotamus on the other. It was a boomerang!

Chapter 8

Rufus's Big Escape

"Hello?" called Rufus, hoping to meet the mystery person who had saved him. But nobody replied. "Hello?" he repeated. "I could do with a little help getting out of here."

Suddenly, he saw a patch of light illuminating the tunnel only a metre or so in front of him. It was coming from the left. Rufus hurried forward to see where the light was coming from.

He saw a turning into a tunnel he hadn't noticed before. He wondered how he could have missed it. Perhaps it had been unlit or perhaps something had blocked its entrance.

"Hello?" Rufus called, again.

Still his rescuer did not reply.

Rufus couldn't wait any longer. One angry troll might have been knocked out, but there were plenty more where he came from. Rufus hurried along the tunnel. After a few strides he saw something that he hadn't thought he'd ever see again – real daylight. He was going to escape from the troll lair!

Eagerly, he followed the tunnel to its exit. He found himself on a ledge on the hillside. He stopped to take a deep breath of fresh air. Then, he climbed down onto the forest floor.

It was thick with ferns and stinging nettles but a path ahead had been trodden. It was a rather wide path and Rufus knew why. There were troll prints everywhere.

Not wanting to take his chances with the nettles, Rufus decided to follow the path. He would just have to keep a lookout for any trolls that were having the same idea.

The path took him to a small clearing. From here, the route away from the caves was much harder to spot. There were three or four paths leading away from the clearing and none of them as well-trodden as the one he arrived from.

He looked around. There were fir trees everywhere. He had no idea which way would take him out of the forest. He was well and truly lost.

But then Rufus noticed that there was more light coming from the lower land. He assumed that must be the fastest way out of the forest. He began running towards the light. He couldn't see the ground below because it was overgrown with plant life. The weeds crunched underfoot.

Suddenly, Rufus found it difficult to run. There was something sticky underfoot. He looked down and realised that he'd trodden in dung! And by the smell of it, it must be troll dung! He dug out his foot and began running again.

Three steps later, *squish!*

More troll dung.

Rufus stepped to the side. *Squish!*

Finally, he managed to find a spot free of dung. He carried on for a few more steps.

Another *squish!*

Rufus looked around him wondering how he could cross the land without stepping on the ground. To his delight, he saw that he beneath an ancient oak.

He grabbed onto its lowest branch and swung himself forward. He swung over the sticky, stinky troll dung, and landed on firm ground.

In only a few minutes, he heard water. He was near the Muckygush! He hurried through the last of the trees until he found himself on the riverbank. Rufus recognised the building on the other side of the river – it was his own house!

Rufus, being much more intelligent than a troll, knew that he would not be able to fly across the river using his arms as wings. He also knew that it would not be safe to swim in so deep a river with dangerous currents and hungry crocodiles.

However, he did know another way to cross the Muckygush. If he followed the water upstream, he would eventually get to a footbridge that would take him safely to the other side. He could them double back on himself and get home.

Rufus began jogging upstream. It felt strange seeing Sludgeside from this side of the river. The town side was covered in houses and pretty, tidy gardens. The Fusty Forest side was covered in gnarly trees, wild ferns and logs that the stormy winter had torn from the trees.

To his horror, Rufus realised that one of the logs ahead was not that at all, but a hungry, threatening crocodile!

Rufus froze. He had forgotten that the

shallower bank on this side of the river meant the dangerous crocs could come and go as they pleased.

He didn't know what to do. He must pass the crocodile to get to safety, but if he got too close, he might be snapped up for dinner.

Rufus thought about heading downstream but he didn't know how far the next bridge was, and it would soon be getting dark. The Fusty Forest was even more dangerous by night than it was by day. He had to pass the crocodile.

Snap! Rufus had stepped on a delicate twig.

The crocodile heard. It began crawling towards Rufus with a greedy glint in its eyes.

Rufus darted for the nearest sycamore tree. The lowest branches were a little too high for him to reach easily, but with a running jump he managed to grab onto a branch and pull himself up. Quickly, he climbed onto the next branch up, to ensure that he was out of reach of the crocodile.

The creature lingered by the base of the trunk, waiting for his prey. What could poor Rufus do? He couldn't get down from the tree without being eaten, but he couldn't stay up the sycamore tree forever.

Then, he noticed that the branch above

him touched a branch from the neighbouring horse chestnut tree. If he could climb from one tree to the next, then he could hop over the top of the crocodile to safety.

Using a smaller branch as a foothold, he managed to climb up onto the higher branch. He was very high up now and falling could break his bones. He had to be very careful.

The branch bowed under Rufus's weight. He felt himself starting to slide. Quickly, he grabbed the branch of the horse chestnut tree. He quickly crawled along the branch, away from the crocodile.

However, when he reached the trunk of the horse chestnut tree, he looked down and found that the lower branches were much farther away than he expected. He could not easily get down.

Rufus gripped onto the bark with his hands and the soles of his shoes. At first, he managed to lower himself slowly down the trunk.

Suddenly, he felt himself slide! He lost grip with his hands and fell, at speed, down the trunk.

Rufus dropped onto the ground with a *bump!* His bottom hurt from the landing but nothing felt broken. He remembered the crocodile. He picked himself up and began to run.

The crocodile started to follow him, but the logs and craggy rocks held him back. After a few paces, it gave up and crawled back into the Muckygush. Thank goodness!

However, Rufus did not stop running. He did not stop running until he got to the footbridge. He crossed the bridge and then crumpled onto the path. He sat there for some moments, catching his breath.

He knew that he was lucky to be alive. He had managed to navigate the Fusty Forest, troll dung and a hungry crocodile alone. However, he would not even have got out of the caves if it hadn't been for the troll hunter.

The troll hunter had saved him – first, by hitting his attacker with a boomerang and then by showing him a safe route out of the lair. Rufus wondered who the troll hunter could be.

* * *

Rufus Sebbleford was late for school the following day. His ordeal with the trolls had left him exhausted and he had overslept. His parents hadn't noticed because it was the semi-final of *Breakfast on Ice*. This meant that he didn't get a chance to tell Polly about the encounter until break time. He sat on his chair, rocking backwards and forwards with a mixture of excitement and fear.

Bruno was now a permanent fixture at their table, so even when Mr Crimplemop turned his back, Rufus still didn't get a chance to talk to Polly alone. Bruno appeared to be wearing a new uniform. It was still handmade and somewhat irregular but at least this one was made from fabric and not newspaper. He had also stopped eating stationery and climbing on the furniture. He did glue his fingers to his ear, but only once, so he was making progress.

Finally, the hands on the clock struck half past ten. Ten agonising seconds passed before the teacher finally announced break time. Rufus sprang out of his seat and beckoned for Polly to follow. However, when she did, Bruno came after her.

Rufus was torn. On the one hand, he wanted to make the new boy feel welcome, but on the other, he didn't trust him well enough to tell him about the trolls. Rufus fingered the boomerang in his coat pocket, still wondering who had thrown it.

"Bruno," said Rufus, "there are some mini eggs in my bag. If you go back inside and fetch the packet then you can have them."

"I haven't got a frying pan," replied Bruno.

"You don't cook mini eggs. They're made of chocolate!"

"Ooh, lovely. Thank you!" said Bruno. Then he remembered that he was trying to blend in with the human children. "Actually, I'm on a diet."

Rufus wanted to tell Bruno that he didn't need to diet but looking at the new boy's belly popping out of his shirt, he was worried for his friend's health. He couldn't pretend that being so overweight was good for him.

He couldn't wait any longer. Rufus had to tell Polly about the trolls. Telling her in front of Bruno wasn't ideal, but he couldn't think of an effective way to get Polly alone.

"I was captured by a troll!" he blurted, excitably.

Polly froze.

Bruno looked away.

"I went back to the bumpy bridge by the crooked church and I thought I saw something in the trees upstream. So, I followed the stream, and that's when a big, fat troll caught me!"

"Are you all right?" asked Polly. "It didn't hurt you did it?"

"I'm fine now," explained Rufus. "A few

bruises from when Gunkfreak dropped me on the floor of their cave, but ..."

"You were inside their cave?" gasped Polly. "And who is Gunkfreak?"

Rufus shuddered.

Bruno shuddered.

"Gunkfreak," explained Rufus, "seems to be one of the most aggressive trolls of all! He's the one who caught me."

"How did you get away?" Polly asked him again.

"It was a troll hunter," Rufus speculated. "The troll hunter threw a boomerang at him."

"Have you still got the boomerang?" asked Bruno, quickly.

"Yes," replied Rufus, reaching into his coat pocket and running his finger along its wooden surface.

Bruno grinned.

"There's nothing to smile about!" remarked Rufus. "The trolls are planning to attack our school!"

"No!" exclaimed Polly.

"They don't have a cunning plan yet," explained Rufus. "Trolls seem to be ... well ... stupid."

Bruno scowled.

Rufus continued, "But it's only a matter of

time before they come up with a sensible plan. The Ogre of Uggle seems to be cleverer than the rest."

"Who is The Ogre of Uggle?" asked Polly.

This time, Bruno spoke. "He's the most feared troll of all – half troll, half giant."

Rufus and Polly stared at the new boy.

"How did you know that?" asked Rufus.

Bruno panicked. He had forgotten that he was supposed to be pretending to be human. "Er ... Um ... I read it in a book!" he fibbed.

Both Rufus and Polly found this rather odd. Bruno had been unable to read his own name that morning. How could he have read a book about The Ogre of Uggle? Still, if there were a book about trolls, Rufus wanted to read it.

"What's the book called?" asked Rufus.

"I can't remember," said Bruno.

"Is that where you learnt what trolls look like?" asked Polly, remembering Bruno's plasticine model.

Bruno's tongue couldn't find the strength to lie again. He hated being dishonest especially towards his friends. Eventually, he managed to bring himself to nod, gently.

"What else did it say in the book?" asked Rufus. "Did it say anything about troll hunters?"

Bruno shook his head.

"The school!" Polly reminded him. "What are we going to do about our school?"

"I don't know yet," admitted Rufus.

"We should call the police!" suggested Polly.

"Do you think they would believe us?" asked Rufus.

"No point," Bruno told them. "You can't put a troll in jail. Trolls can bend iron bars with their bare hands."

"Yikes!" gasped Polly.

The bell started to ring. Time to go back into school. Now, having spoken to Bruno, Rufus had even more questions running through his head.

"You have to tell Mr Crimplemop," Polly told Rufus, as they walked towards the door. "If trolls are going to attack the school, then the teachers need to be made aware."

"Do you really think so?" asked Rufus.

"Yes!" said Polly. "It's all very well wanting to be a troll hunter, Rufus, but you can't take on dozens of trolls all by yourself."

"Twelve and a half," said Bruno.

"Huh?"

"There are twelve and a half bad trolls in

Sludgeside. I er ... read about them in my book."

"How can there be twelve and a half trolls?" asked Rufus.

"Twelve actual trolls plus The Ogre of Uggle. Like I said, he's half troll, half giant."

Polly looked thoughtful. "We're going to need reinforcements."

Rufus remembered Mr Crimplemop telling him that he had an overactive imagination. Is that what he would say this time? Rufus didn't particularly want to be told that he was deluded, but if twelve and a half trolls were going to attack the school, then it was his duty to tell his teacher.

He waited until the other children had gone inside, thankful that most of them had no idea about the looming danger.

"Hurry up, Rufus!" called Mr Crimplemop.

"Sir?"

"Yes, Rufus."

"I need to talk to you."

"About what?"

"Trolls."

The teacher smiled to himself. "I haven't got time now. Class is about to resume."

"But sir ..."

"No buts, Rufus!"

"They are going to attack the school!"

The teacher turned and faced Rufus. "What?"

"I overheard Gunkfreak talking to the other trolls. They plan to attack our school and eat all the children! What do you think I should do?"

"Perhaps, Rufus, you should write a story book."

Just as he feared, Mr Crimplemop didn't believe him. Twelve and a half angry trolls were going to attack Sludgeside School and it was down to the three ten years olds to stop them.

Chapter 9

A Remarkable Discovery

Dinner at the Super-Troll-Knobbly-Foot house was an interesting affair. Ma had successfully signed on, and the government was helping her with money for food and rent. However, having never set foot inside a supermarket before, Ma didn't understand how to shop for groceries.

Today, she served up a bowl of washing-up-liquid soup with a chocolate muffin smeared in mustard. Bruno and his sisters found it revolting, but they were still so happy not to be stealing sheep and goats anymore that they gobbled it all up. Of course, such food would make a human very poorly, but trolls have very strong bellies.

Ma got up to fetch some custard to top up

their glasses. Bruno noticed that she was walking differently from usual. She appeared to be balancing on two sticks.

"What are those?" asked Bruno.

"Crutches," explained Ma.

"What are crutches?"

"Help me bad leg," she replied.

Bruno watched as his mum got around the kitchen with ease. He hadn't seen her move that fast since before her unfortunate hula hooping accident.

"That's amazing!" said Bruno.

"Yarb," agreed Ma.

Then, Ma proudly told her children about the *new* new uniforms she had made for them. She explained that she was really getting the hang of sewing – it was her hidden talent! She told them that the Mark 3 uniform looked every bit as good as a shop-bought uniform. She was settling into human life well. She had even learnt that four pigtails were too many for a little girl and now, she only parted the twins' hair into three pigtails each.

Finally, when they reached their course of after dinner toilet rolls, Bruno approached the subject of Gunkfreak's plan to attack the school.

"Gunkfreak kidnapped a boy from my

class," he explained.

"Gosh!" cried Betty.

"Golly!" said Belinda.

"Goblin!" exclaimed Ma.

"Fortunately, he managed to escape," Bruno continued, keeping his own part in that secret.

"Phew!" said the others.

"However, not before he overheard Gunkfreak plotting an evil plan to attack our school!"

"That's dreadful!" squealed Betty.

"I thought we had finally seen the back of that brute, Gunkfreak," exclaimed Belinda.

"Treble!" remarked Ma.

"I think she means 'terrible'," whispered Belinda.

"My words be better!" pleaded Ma.

"You're right mum," said Bruno, kindly. "You have been getting much better at using words."

Ma looked pleased with herself.

"Now," began Bruno, "how are we going to stop the trolls attacking our school?"

"Yer not," said Ma, firmly.

"Why not?" asked the three others.

"Because we need to be indigo!" explained Ma.

"I think you mean 'incognito'," Bruno pointed out.

"What does 'incognito' mean?" asked Betty.

"It means disguised or undercover," Bruno told them. "Mum is trying to remind us that we have to pretend to be human. Isn't that right?"

"Yarb!" replied Ma. "Protect secret!"

"My friend Rufus is human and he is going to be a troll hunter when he grows up."

The others gasped.

"He won't hurt us! Only the disgusting ones that we don't like either. They *are* planning to attack our school! We would have a chance of standing up to Gunkfreak and the others, while pretending to be human," explained Bruno.

"Won't work!" barked Ma.

"Mum's right," said Betty. "The people at our school may be fooled by hats, fake tan and bubble gum but Gunkfreak would recognise us right away."

"He might not," argued Belinda. "He is very stupid."

"Agreed," said Bruno. "But we can't take that risk. If another troll recognises me in front of a human, the game will be up. We would have to go back to living in that smelly cave and stealing farm animals for our dinner."

The others shuddered. They had been living in a house for less than a week and already they knew it was right for them. The Super-Troll-Knobbly-Foot family were not like other trolls – they were thoughtful, moral and sophisticated. Ma bit the lid off a tube of toothpaste and started sucking minty paste from the tube. Well, they were sophisticated *for trolls*.

"If only we could stand up to Gunkfreak without getting recognised ..." continued Bruno.

"We small!" shouted Ma.

"She's right," agreed Belinda. "We can't stand up to a troll like Gunkfreak. We are the smallest trolls in the cave."

"There are twelve and a half of them," Betty pointed out. "And they are all much bigger than us."

"But my friends Rufus and Polly are very smart," insisted Bruno. "Sometimes brains can be more powerful than size or numbers."

"Must not tell um!" boomed Ma.

"Of course I won't tell any humans that I am a troll," Bruno assured her. "But I am going to offer to help my friends. My knowledge of the caves and trolls might be useful to them."

"We'll help too!" offered Betty.

Belinda nodded, enthusiastically.

They looked at Ma. She frowned. Her children gazed at her with their big, charming hazel eyes. Eventually she sighed and then nodded. "Yarb," she agreed. "Me help."

* * *

Bruno decided to try to find Rufus first. He thought that the telephone was for drying wet feet and didn't know you could make calls from it, so he had to go to Rufus's house to talk to him. But then he realised that he didn't know where Rufus lived. He did, however, know where Polly lived.

He went up to his bedroom to find his hat, and saw the new clothes that his mum had made. They were incredible. In addition to a replica school uniform, she had made him a pair of jeans and a t-shirt with an alien on it. He loved his new clothes.

So, he put on the new jeans, t-shirt and his hat, checked his fake tan in the mirror, and grabbed some bubble gum to disguise his spit. Then he hurried down the road to find Polly. He would ask Polly to show him where Rufus lived.

* * *

Rufus Sebbleford's head was a mess. In the last forty-eight hours he'd met a very peculiar new boy, been kidnapped by a troll and learned of said troll's intentions to attack his school.

He wandered past the park and recognised two girls playing on the swings. They were Bruno's little sisters, Betty and Belinda. They were swinging with great excitement, as if they'd never played on swings before.

Rufus would have stopped to say hello, but he needed to see Polly. There were so many mysteries to talk through, and so many plans to make. Thank goodness he had a good friend that he could talk to about such things.

However, when he arrived at Polly's house, he was in for a surprise. He walked along the grey terrace and found the Chromatics' plastic door. But when he rang the doorbell, Polly's mum told him that Polly was already out, *with Bruno*!

Rufus felt his face flush red. Polly and Bruno had gone out without him? How could they? He was their friend too!

Suddenly, all of the things that he found weird about Bruno started to annoy him – his orange skin, his faintly whiffy body odour, his stupid hat ... What sort of religion was

Hopscotchism anyway? It didn't sound like a religion to him. And how could a boy who couldn't read have read about The Ogre of Uggle in a book?

Rufus stormed back towards his house. He stamped past the crooked church and over the bumpy bridge. He thundered past the shops. Just as he was about to march past the playground, he noticed something odd. One of the twins was dangling upside down from the monkey bar, and her hat had fallen off. Rufus looked more closely. *Jeepers creepers!* The little girl had horns!

The ten-year-old-boy stared in disbelief. Betty Trolley was not a seven-year-old girl after all – she was a troll! But if Betty was a troll, then Belinda must be a troll. And if Betty and Belinda were both trolls then ...

Rufus felt all of his blood rush to his head. He felt faint. The Trolley family were trolls! Bruno Trolley was a troll! This was no time for fainting. He had to find Polly. She could be in great danger!

He began to run, hoping that the twins hadn't noticed him gawping at Betty's horns. But where should he run to? Where would Bruno have taken Polly? Would he have taken her back to the troll cave? Rufus remembered learning landmarks as Gunkfreak carried him, trying to memorise the route. Could he recall it?

Would it be enough to barge into the cave with just his pocket troll hunting kit? Probably not. He reached into his coat pocket. The boomerang was still there, but Rufus did not know how to throw a boomerang. No, this was a time for his bow and arrow.

Although going back to his den to pick up his bow and arrow would lose time, he knew that he couldn't ambush the troll cave without it. If he was going to stand a chance of saving Polly, then he needed his best weapon. He remembered the night when he was five years, three-hundred and sixty-four days old, and how the troll hunter had saved him with an arrow. Now it was his turn to be a troll-hunting archer.

Rufus gulped. He had liked Bruno. Certainly, he was a strange boy but he had seemed a good friend. He didn't want to have to kill him. But then Rufus reminded himself that Bruno was not a little boy after all, but a troll. For all he knew, Bruno could be a spy helping Gunkfreak with his plan to attack the school.

As fast as his legs could carry him, Rufus

hurried home. He dashed up the garden path, rushed in through the front door, bounded in through the house, dashed past his parents watching television, and then sprinted to his den at the bottom of the garden.

He threw open the door. But what he saw before him gave him an almighty shock – Bruno and Polly were sitting down in his den, enjoying cups of lemonade.

Chapter 10

A Risky and Very Silly Plan

Rufus rushed inside his den and grabbed Bruno. He tried to immobilise him by wrapping his arms around him but trolls are fat and Rufus's arms only reached his sides.

"Rufus!" cried Polly. "What on earth are you doing to poor Bruno?"

"He's not 'poor Bruno' – he's a troll!" shouted Rufus.

"What?" laughed Polly, in disbelief.

"It's true!" exclaimed Rufus. "I saw Betty's hat fall off. She has horns! They're not Hopscotchists, they're trolls!"

"That's ridiculous!" scoffed Polly.

Rufus reached for Bruno's hat. Bruno ducked but Rufus closed in on him and tugged the hat clean off his head.

Polly stared, in horror, at two stubby little horns protruding from Bruno's forehead.

"And I bet, if we get his shoes off we'll find that his feet only have four toes!" cried Rufus. He grabbed one of Bruno's legs and tried to pull off his shoe.

Bruno hopped around on one leg. "It's not what you think!" he pleaded.

"You *are* a troll!" cried Polly, backing away. She reached for Rufus's bow and arrow.

"Please don't hurt me!" cried Bruno. "I'm good!"

"A likely story!" snorted Rufus. "You're a *troll*!"

"It was me who saved you!" Bruno tried to explain. "I threw that boomerang."

"You're making this up!" shouted Rufus, still tugging at the shoe. Bruno wobbled and hopped like a chicken on a pogo stick.

"It has a sausage carved into one side and a hippopotamus on the other!" Bruno told Rufus, trying not to fall over.

Rufus stopped in his tracks. The boomerang in his pocket *did* have the peculiar carvings. And he had never actually shown it to Bruno, so he must have seen it before. Rufus let Bruno's foot drop to the floor. Bruno wobbled and fell backwards onto his bottom.

"That doesn't mean that you threw it," replied Rufus.

"I did throw it!" pleaded Bruno, picking himself up. "Gobb Podgeleton had you cornered. I knocked him out with the boomerang, then I opened a tunnel, which led you out to the hillside."

Rufus was stunned. Bruno must have been the one that saved him. He hadn't told anybody about the exit tunnel.

"So ..." asked Rufus, trembling, "... there are good trolls as well as bad?"

"Only a few," explained Bruno. "And we have only just turned properly good. We decided that we would live as humans because your government helps struggling families. Trolls don't even have a government. We just have The Ogre of Uggle, and he doesn't care if we starve. We had to steal sheep and goats to survive. Please don't tell anybody what we really are, or we will have to go back to a life of crime!"

"Gosh!" gasped Polly.

"Our real name is Super-Troll-Knobbly-Foot, but we go by Trolley to sound more human," Bruno continued.

"*Troll*ey! Of course!" said Polly. "You said

it was Trolley like a supermarket trolley, but actually it's Trolly, as in troll!"

"It's not the most subtle name," blushed Bruno, "But I had to think on the spot."

Rufus didn't know what to say. Eventually, he managed to ask, "But what were you doing in my den?"

"We were looking for you!" Polly told him.

"It's a fantastic den!" raved Bruno. "And so well disguised. I had no idea that there was anything here besides trees and bushes!"

"That's the idea," said Rufus, proudly.

Noticing that Rufus was softening, Bruno begged, "Please don't tell anybody that my family are trolls!"

Rufus thought about it. People might not understand that Bruno was a good troll. Already people like Anita Grumblenose and Barry Blither had been rude because he was a little different. If they knew that he was a different species, they would be even more horrid. What if Bruno was right? – what if his family really would have to go back to an unsavoury troll lifestyle?

"All right. I'll keep your secret," agreed Rufus.

"Me too!" added Polly.

Bruno grinned. "Do you promise?"

"We promise," they chorused.

"Thank you!" said Bruno, almost crying with joy. "My mum and my sisters want to help you stop Gunkfreak. We don't want to give away our identities, but we will do anything else we can to help."

Rufus thought about it. Until now, he had assumed that every troll was bad, but Bruno had saved his life. Plus, Polly had been alone with Bruno and was still perfectly safe. If Bruno had wanted to eat her, he could have done. Obviously, he had not.

"In what ways could you help?" asked Rufus.

"I know the Fusty Forest like the back of my hand," said Bruno.

Rufus looked at the back of Bruno's hand – it was hairy and warty, not unlike a forest.

"Also," continued Bruno. "I know about troll weaknesses."

"Such as?" asked Polly.

"They are very stupid. My sisters and me, we're cleverer than most, because our father is Marv the Magnificent – the cleverest troll in the land."

"Can't we get his help?" asked Rufus.

"Nobody has seen him for years. Some people think he ran off, others think he's ..."

Bruno gulped, "… dead."

"And what do you think?" asked Polly, softly.

"I don't know," admitted Bruno, sadly. "Some days I'm sure he'll come back. Other days, I'm not so sure."

Polly touched Bruno gently on the shoulder.

"Anything else we should know about trolls?" asked Rufus, taking a seat.

"Trolls sleep during the day."

"You don't," observed Polly.

"Only because I am trying to live like a human. I used to come out only at night."

"But Gunkfreak was out during daylight," Rufus pointed out. "It was afternoon when he kidnapped me."

"He was surveying your school," explained Bruno. "Gunkfreak usually sleeps by day."

"Anything else?" asked Polly, handing around some fresh lemonade.

"They like to eat little girls," explained Bruno.

"Have you ever …" began Polly, then trailed off.

"Never. Only sheep and goats."

Polly relaxed a little.

"But I'm a boy," Rufus pointed out. "And

one tried to eat me!"

"Trolls eat little boys but they prefer little girls. To a troll, a boy tastes like a savoury dish, such as a pie or a salad. But little girls taste like pudding, such as a chocolate brownie, an ice cream or a jelly."

Polly shuddered.

Rufus took out a notebook. "So: 1. They're stupid. 2. They sleep during the day. 3. They prefer to eat little girls to little boys. Anything else?"

"Smelly feet," added Bruno.

"Smelly feet?" echoed the others, giggling.

Rufus wrote, "4. Trolls have smelly feet."

"Narb, narb, narb," laughed Bruno. "They don't *have* smelly feet. They *like* smelly feet."

"Ugh!" gasped Polly.

"Disgusting!" remarked Rufus.

"A troll can never resist the stench of smelly feet. Whenever a troll smells a smelly foot, it will drop whatever it's doing to investigate."

"But if trolls like smelly feet, why do they prefer to eat girls? Boys are much smellier than girls!"

"Oi!" said Rufus.

"Well, you are!" laughed Polly.

"Trolls prefer to eat girls but they are

harder to find, because they are less stinky," Bruno told them.

Rufus added, '4. Trolls like smelly feet' to his list.

"But how are we going to stop a bunch of stupid trolls who like smelling boys, eating little girls and only come out at night?" asked Polly.

"I've got it!" cried Rufus.

"What?"

"We find the smelliest boys in Sludgeside ..."

"Yes?"

"Then we steal their shoes ..."

"And?"

"We make a big pile of smelly shoes far away on the other side of the hills, and all the trolls will move away, to be near the shoes."

Bruno looked thoughtful. Then, he replied glumly, "That won't work, I'm afraid."

"Why not?"

"The trolls would certainly go searching for the smell, but as soon as they realised it was just a pile of shoes, they would shake their fists and go back to the caves."

"What if we draw the trolls out with the smelly shoes, and then we shoot them with bows and arrows?" suggested Rufus.

Bruno looked sad for a moment.

"What's the matter?" asked Rufus.

"I used to know somebody who had a bow and arrow, that's all," he muttered.

"What do you think of my plan?" asked Rufus.

"An arrow wouldn't kill a troll, only stun it," explained Bruno. "Troll skin is tough and our layers of fat are self-healing. That's why we've lasted for centuries without dying out, despite most of us being really, really stupid."

"Is there anything that *can* kill a troll?" asked Rufus.

"Do we have to *kill* them?" asked Polly. "Can't we just put them in a really big pit or something?"

"They tried that in Bumpybogton," Bruno told them. "But the pit slowly filled with troll dung, which dried in the sun, and eventually they walked out."

"Ugh!" gasped Polly. "Why didn't somebody clean out the pit?"

"Would you want to clean a pit of hungry trolls that hadn't eaten human for months?"

"Good point."

"What can kill a troll?" repeated Rufus.

"Water," said Bruno.

"Water?" asked Rufus, surprised. "Can we

attack them with super soakers and water bombs?"

"Narb, not that sort of water. I meant water like lakes and rivers. Trolls can't swim," clarified Bruno.

They thought about it. It made sense – with their big, heavy bodies, trolls certainly did not look buoyant.

"I've got an idea!" sang Polly, grinning. "We build a pile of smelly shoes on this side of the river, then the trolls will come out of their caves and fall into the water."

Bruno looked thoughtful. For a moment Rufus and Polly wondered if they'd finally found a plan that would work.

But eventually Bruno said, "Narb, sorry. The trolls would come out when they smelt the shoes. But they wouldn't risk crossing a river based on smell alone."

"What would they cross a river for?" asked Rufus.

Bruno looked at Polly.

"Me?" she asked.

"Little girls," said Bruno.

"I'm not that little – I'm ten!" protested Polly, indignant. Then, she looked thoughtful. "What if we made a really big pile of smelly shoes to draw the trolls out? Then, I'll stand at the bottom of the garden. The trolls will try to cross the river to get to me, and drown!"

"Yarb!" exclaimed Bruno. "That's perfect! That's exactly what we need to do."

"No," said Rufus, firmly.

"What?" asked the other two, surprised.

"It's too dangerous. I won't let you do it," he told Polly.

"But I want to!" she declared.

"I won't let you. There must be another way."

"There is no other way," said Polly.

"Actually," thought Rufus. "There is another way!"

"What way?" asked Polly and Bruno, in unison.

"It's risky and very silly," he told them.

"What is it?"

"It involves coloured ribbons, pretty dresses, really big mirrors, and very, very stinky shoes."

Chapter 11

Stinky Shoe Selection

The next morning at school, Rufus, Polly and Bruno could not concentrate. All they could think about was their plan, particularly stage one, which could be executed as soon as break time arrived. They were so focused that Bruno didn't even eat any pencil shavings or Blu-Tack.

Mr Crimplemop watched them intently. He could sense that they were excited about something, but he didn't know what. He hoped that Rufus wasn't filling people's heads with his far-fetched theory that trolls were planning to attack the school. If the wrong people were told, it could cause an enormous panic.

Eventually, break time came. The three

friends quietly filed out into the playground, so as not to arouse suspicion. But Mr Crimplemop noticed that they were unusually quiet and instantly wondered what they were up to.

Once in the yard, the three hurried around to the side of the school and tried the side door. Alas, it was locked. Their hearts sank. How would they be able to get the supplies that they needed if they couldn't get back inside the school? And they couldn't go back in through the front door without being spotted.

Then Bruno noticed that a window was open. However, the window was about eight feet off the ground. "Maybe if I stood on your shoulders ..." he began, looking at Rufus.

"Trust me, trolls and small windows don't mix," Rufus told him, remembering that night he had first seen a troll. Bruno was far too big to fit through without hurting himself. Rufus also suspected that it could be somewhat painful having somebody built like a potato filled with rocks, on your shoulders.

Rufus, on the other hand, would be skinny enough to squeeze through. "Maybe, if you stood on my shoulders, you could climb in through the window?" suggested Bruno.

Rufus looked at Bruno; he was big but not tall. "Probably not. But perhaps if Polly stands on your shoulders and I stand on Polly's ..."

"Quick!" said Polly. "I think that could work, but we'll have to act fast in case somebody catches us."

Polly leapt up onto Bruno's shoulders. He was solid and she found him easy to balance upon. Polly, on the other hand, made a much wobblier perch. Bruno made a step with his hands, which helped Rufus get high enough to climb onto Polly's shoulders. However, he couldn't get his balance. He wobbled and fell, crashing into the playground!

Smack.

"Are you all right?" asked his friends, alarmed.

Already, brave Rufus was busy trying to climb up once again. "I'm fine."

This time, he was successful. He managed to balance on Polly's shoulders just long enough to grab onto the window frame. He used his arms to pull him up and slipped in through the window.

He found himself in the locker room, surrounded by pegs with coats and bags hanging from them. It had that smell of damp P.E. kits.

Rufus hurried to the side door and opened it, letting Bruno and Polly inside.

"We did it!" squeaked Polly.

"It's not over yet," Rufus warned her. He removed three empty bin sacks, which he had kept rolled up in his pocket, and handed one to each of his friends. "Now come on, grab!"

Polly grabbed the nearest P.E. kit and gave it an almighty sniff. "Yuck!" she cried, coughing and spluttering. She reached inside, plucked out a pair of smelly trainers and chucked them into her sack.

Rufus began doing to same, only taking more gentle sniffs – he didn't want to inhale large quantities of eau de smelly boy!

Bruno, on the other hand, loved the opportunity to smell some stinky shoes. To him they smelt like melted chocolate.

"Ew! This one's revolting!" cried Rufus, holding up a blue and green canvas bag.

"That's mine!" admitted Bruno, blushing.

"I'm so sorry! I didn't mean ..." stuttered Rufus.

"It's fine," said Bruno. "I *am* a troll. Being stinky goes with the territory."

After a few minutes, they had collectively gathered at least thirty pairs of trainers, ranging from mildly pongy to absolutely disgusting.

Suddenly, they heard the bell. Break time

was over! If they didn't get back to the front door soon Mr Crimplemop might find out that they hadn't stayed in the front yard where they were supposed to be. It wouldn't be long before somebody came looking for them. What if they got caught stinky-shoe-handed?

"We've got to go!" cried Bruno, charging for the door.

"Don't forget your sack!" Polly reminded him.

The three of them dragged the bin sacks full of stinky trainers to the side door. Bruno opened it and they crept out into the alley. They dragged the sacks to the far corner of the backyard where the caretaker stored the rubbish. Then, praying that the second part of their plan would work, they left the sacks and sprinted around to the front of the school.

Mr Crimplemop didn't notice the three trouble makers appear from the wrong side of the school. He did however, notice that they all appeared to be out of breath. He knew that they were up to something, but had no idea what it was.

* * *

Mr Grubstopper had left his favourite pen in his car's glove compartment. He was a man of habit and he simply could not function without his favourite pen. He put down his papers, in a perfectly straight stack, and went out into the school backyard. He marched towards the back gate that led to the car park.

Just as he was about to open the gate, he saw something that took him by surprise. A very wide lady on crutches appeared to be emptying the bins. She had two sacks of rubbish slung over one shoulder and was busy diving into a third bin. She really was very broad and made carrying sacks look like light work. She was dressed most strangely; she appeared to be wearing a yellow plastic dress and had a waste paper basket on her head.

"Excuse me. What are you doing?" he asked.

"Bin lady," she replied.

"I've never seen you before."

"New," she grunted, turning to face him.

Then, the head teacher realised that he *had* seen the peculiar lady before. Her wide nose and orange skin was very distinctive. "It's you, Ma Trolley!" he exclaimed.

"Narb," she said, shaking her head.

Mr Grubstopper would recognise that peculiar grunt anywhere. It *was* Ma Trolley.

"I know it's you," he said. "Why are you

pretending it isn't?"

Ma shrugged. She couldn't tell him that she was here collecting three sacks of stinky shoes in order to drown an entire den of evil, child-eating trolls.

"Are you sure being a bin lady is the right job for you?" Mr Grubstopper asked Ma, looking at her crutches. "I mean, with your bad leg?"

"Don't be disc ... disc ..." Ma struggled with the long word.

"Discriminating?" asked Mr Grubstopper, sounding alarmed.

"Yarb," she said, nodding.

"I'm not discriminating!" he said, horrified. "It just doesn't look easy, moving bin sacks when you're on crutches."

"I be fine," she assured him. Thanks to the crutches, Ma had been able to get out and about in ways she hadn't done in years.

"Where is your dustbin lorry?" asked the head teacher.

Ma didn't know what to say, so instead she started singing a jingle that she'd heard on the telly. "Go compare! Go compare!" And then she slung the final sack over her shoulder and hobbled away as fast as her crutches could carry her.

"What a peculiar woman," thought Mr Grubstopper. Then, he went back to the matter of his favourite pen.

* * *

Rufus knew better than to share any more of his knowledge about trolls with Mr Crimplemop. After his teacher had failed to listen to his intelligence about the school attack, Rufus had given up all hope of being taken seriously.

However, Rufus did need some information and he knew that his teacher was the best person to ask. Mr Crimplemop was the wisest person that he knew.

It was lunchtime and Rufus's classmates had gone to the canteen for lunch. Mr Crimplemop picked up his Mr Splendiferous Science Park mug, looking forward to a lovely cup of relaxing tea.

"Mr Crimplemop?" asked Rufus.

The teacher jumped. "Oh, hello, Rufus. I didn't know that you were still here. Why aren't you in the dinner queue with everybody else?"

"I need to ask you about bendy mirrors."

"Bendy mirrors?"

"Yes. Supposing a ..." Rufus was about to say 'troll' when he thought better of it.

"Supposing a person was nearly one and a half metres tall ..."

"Okay ..."

"What sort of mirror would I need to make it ... I mean *him* look shorter?"

Mr Crimplemop studied Rufus for a while. "What are you plotting?"

"Nothing," lied Rufus.

"Are you sure?" asked the teacher. The twinkle in his eye met the twinkle in Rufus's. The ten-year-old quickly looked away.

"I was just wondering. Supposing some bad ... er ... people wanted to attack a school and there was this plan to stop them ..."

"Couldn't that be very dangerous? Sounds like something best left to the police."

"Not if the baddies were so strong that they could bend iron bars with their bare hands!"

"Rufus, nobody can bend iron bars with their bare hands."

"Well, supposing you couldn't go to the police because one of your friends would get in a lot of trouble and his family would have to return to a life of crime ..."

"Er ... right. Perhaps you could tell your teacher all about it?"

Rufus thought long and hard. He liked Mr Crimplemop and if the teacher *was* ready to listen, he wanted to tell him the truth. However, he had promised Bruno that he would keep his identity a secret. "No, I can't."

"Are you sure?"

"Positive."

"So what did you want to ask me?"

"Supposing you knew you could stop the baddies but your plan involved making them look much smaller than they actually were ..."

Mr Crimplemop studied Rufus for some moments. "A convex mirror would make the baddie look shorter," he explained. "But not the sort we use in class, it would need to be very big – probably at least two metres tall."

"Like the sort you get at the fair or the Mr Splendiferous Science Park?" asked Rufus.

"Exactly," said the teacher, fiddling with his mug.

"Thank you, sir," said Rufus.

The teacher looked thoughtful as he watched Rufus walk away. Just as the boy was about to vanish, Mr Crimplemop called after him. "How many baddies are we talking about?"

"About a dozen. Why do you ask?"

"I just wondered," replied Mr Crimplemop.

Rufus gulped – a dozen stinky, ferocious trolls and it was his job to stop them all.

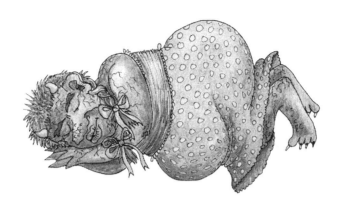

Chapter 12

The Dressing of the Trolls

Rufus and Polly sat with the Trolley family in the living room of their house. The two children were somewhat baffled by the interior – the walls were papered with toilet roll and the carpet was made from moss. Instead of photographs, they had torn up pizza boxes pinned to the wall. 'Ham and Pineapple' hung above the mantelpiece.

"So, we've managed to collect the shoes," Rufus remarked, "but how on earth are we going to get the enormous convex mirrors?"

The others stared back, blankly. Getting the mirrors wasn't the most dangerous part of the plan, but it was proving very tricky. Where on earth were they going to find two-metre tall bendy mirrors?

"A fairground?" suggested Betty.

"There isn't a fair in town at the moment," Rufus pointed out, glumly.

"What about the Mr Splendiferous Science Park?" suggested Polly. "The first time I ever saw a bendy mirror was at the science park."

"But how would we get into the science park?" asked Rufus. "There is a security fence!"

"True," admitted Polly. "If only we knew somebody who worked there. Then we could ask to borrow the mirrors."

"But what could we say?" asked Rufus. "We could hardly tell them that we're planning to use them to kill trolls. They'd laugh at us!"

"I'm sure we could think of something," said Polly. Then she added, thoughtfully, "I wonder how you make a mirror ..."

"With great difficulty," Rufus told her. "We would need a glazier."

"Mirrors are made from ice?" asked Bruno, excitedly.

"No, you're thinking of a *glacier*!" explained Rufus.

"We don't know any glaziers," said Polly. "What are we going to do? Without the mirrors, the plan won't work at all."

They all felt deflated. They had seemed so

close to catching the trolls and saving the other children. Surely an equipment shortage wouldn't stop them.

"How are the outfits coming on?" asked Rufus, changing the subject.

"Yarb!" grunted Ma.

"Spectacular!" added Bruno.

"Can we see them?" asked Polly.

"Noyt!" replied Ma.

"Not yet," translated Bruno. "She wants to wait until they're finished so that you can see the full effect."

Rufus and Polly were disappointed. They couldn't wait to see the costumes that Ma was making. Judging by the beautiful dresses that Betty and Belinda were wearing, she had become an excellent seamstress.

"Will they be finished by Saturday night?" asked Polly.

"Yarb!" replied Ma.

"What's the use of having the costumes ready if we don't have the mirrors?" snapped Rufus. "Without the mirrors, we have no chance."

* * *

Rufus arrived home feeling decidedly glum. His mum was watching 'Strictly Come Re-design my Shed' on the telly while his dad used his smartphone to browse new home entertainment systems. Rufus decided not to talk to them. He felt too grumpy. Instead, he went straight out to his den where he could be alone. He stomped down the garden. However, as he approached his den, he saw something glittering in the light.

He could feel his heart pounding as he approached. Could he see what he thought he could see? It looked like a row of mirrors!

Sure enough, laid out on the grass in front of him were twelve two-metre convex mirrors. Enough to make a whole wall of mirrors!

Rufus tried to lift one. It was heavier than he had expected. Eventually, using all his might, he managed to prop one up against a tree. He looked at his reflection – tiny! These mirrors were perfect! They were exactly what he needed to trap the trolls. But where had they come from?

* * *

Saturday arrived. Rufus dressed himself in his best camouflage outfit – green cargo pants and a black t-shirt. He put on a black knitted hat to hide his vibrant red hair. He put on his plimsolls because they had the softest soles and would therefore be the quietest. Yes, his heart pounded. It was the most exciting mission of his life. Tonight, he would be a true troll hunter.

Polly pulled on her only pair of dark jeans and a green camouflage t-shirt that she had borrowed from Rufus. She tied her hair back with a green pipe cleaner. She was both nervous and excited at the same time. The only trolls she'd ever met were the Trolley family and they were good trolls. She wondered what a bad troll would be like.

Bruno got his beige troll cloth out of the cupboard. He had hoped he'd never have to wear it again, but tonight he had to look as though he'd given up pretending to be human. He had to look as if he had decided to return to a life of trolling. That way, if any of the trolls saw him, they would think he was on their side. They were less likely to hurt an ally.

Ma and the twins did the same. They looked at their reflections and realised how far they'd come in just a short time. Only a week before, they'd been grubby trolls and now they had a house, food that was paid for and, most importantly, friends. They might not like wearing the troll cloths but they only had to do it one more time and then never again.

"Are you sure you want to come?" Bruno had asked Ma ten times. "You've still got a bad leg."

Ma kept swinging from her crutches, showing Bruno how mobile she had become and demonstrating that she had no intention of staying at home.

That afternoon, Rufus and Polly met at the bumpy bridge by the crooked church. They couldn't meet the Trolley family in a built-up area now that they were dressed like trolls. The two friends greeted each other quietly. Both knew the danger they were about to put themselves in but they both recognised that putting themselves in danger was necessary to save the school.

They followed the stream towards the woods, past the broken scooter and the damp, slug-covered armchair. As they got to the thick fir trees, Rufus shivered, remembering the moment when Gunkfreak 'had captured him at this exact spot. He looked around him. The area should be safe now because Bruno and his family should be here.

As they crept into the Fusty Forest, Rufus and Polly began to wonder where the Trolley family were. "They should be here by now," whispered Rufus.

"They will be," Polly assured him.

"Where are they, then?" asked Rufus, wondering if Bruno had got cold feet about turning on his own kind.

Just then, a figure crept out of the darkness. Rufus leapt, thinking it was Gunkfreak. He almost didn't recognise Bruno. Without his fake tan and human clothes, he looked alarmingly similar to the bad trolls. However, when Rufus looked more closely, he could see that Bruno had kind eyes and softer skin.

"All right, buddy?" asked Bruno, sensing Rufus's discomfort.

Polly just stood and stared, mouth open. Certainly, Bruno looked a little scarier than usual, but in a funny way, she preferred his greenish skin. It was the real him. It was honest.

"We'd better get moving," suggested Bruno. "We've got a lot to do before dusk."

"True," agreed Rufus. "Where are the others?"

Ma and Betty stepped out from behind nearby trees. Like Bruno's, their skin had a greenish tinge. Rather than troll cloths tied around their waists, they were wearing what appeared to be grubby pillowcases with holes cut for their arms and head. They each carried a sack of supplies for the mission.

"We didn't want to scare you by all jumping out at once," explained Bruno.

"Who's scared?" asked Polly. "Nice horns!" she added.

Rufus rolled his eyes. He remembered that Polly hadn't had the same experiences as him. She hadn't faced nearly being gobbled by a troll when she was five years, three-hundred and sixty-four days old. She hadn't been kidnapped by the hideous Gunkfreak. Perhaps once she'd seen the pure horror of the troll cave, those horns would give her the same chill they gave him.

Ma led the way into to the forest and the troupe followed, looking around as they pressed forward in case villains were hiding in the trees.

"Don't worry, trolls don't usually come out during the day," Bruno reminded them.

"Except Gunkfreak," gulped Rufus.

"That was a rare occurrence. We're probably fine," Polly remarked.

"'Probably' isn't good enough!" snapped Rufus.

"You knew there would be risks," Polly pointed out.

"True," agreed Rufus. "It's a dangerous mission, but it has to be done."

Rufus felt himself getting out of breath as the path inclined upwards. He knew that they were getting near the caves. He felt afraid, but he reminded himself that he had to be brave if he wanted to be a proper troll hunter.

"Haree!" grunted Ma.

"Here we are," translated Bruno.

"But I thought you said we were going to a cave," said Polly. "There's nothing here but a cliff."

Ma began shoving a rock. She was large, but Polly doubted that she was big enough to move a boulder like that. However, the stone suddenly dislodged, opening the entrance to what appeared to be a rather large cave. A waft of sprouts, rotting cabbages and fetid egg blew from the cave. It smelt like a dustbin buffet. Polly found herself spluttering.

The six moved forward timidly. The trolls *should* be asleep, but what if they weren't? There were twelve and a half trolls, each one bigger than any one of the good guys.

"I be going first," Ma insisted.

She crept inside. The others peered into the cave. There appeared to be five gigantic, mouldy potatoes lying on the ground.

Ma approached one of the potatoes. On closer inspection, it was clearly a troll fast asleep. Polly gasped, having never seen the full horror of a bad troll before. She was surprised by how ugly it was – not just unpleasant, but downright revolting. She looked at Bruno and wondered how he could be related to such a disagreeable-looking creature.

Rufus recognised the troll. It was the one with the snotty moustache. "I've seen him before," he whispered.

"That's Tash," Bruno told him.

"Because of the moustache?" asked Rufus, knowingly.

"No," explained Bruno. "It's short for Natasha."

"Wait! That's a *woman*?" asked Rufus, looking at the troll's hairy upper lip with astonishment.

Ma attempted to walk on tippy toes to be extra quiet. However, trolls are so round, and their feet so lumpy, that they find it hard to balance on their toes. Even with her crutches, she wobbled and slipped, landing on sleeping Tash!

The others gasped. They couldn't risk getting spotted! Would Tash wake up and find them here?

Tash snorted, causing an earth shaking rumble, then rolled over and went back to sleep.

The others relaxed, slightly.

Ma, now recognising that it was better to walk on flat feet, trotted over to the next troll. She leant over him and nodded to the others.

"He's asleep," Bruno explained.

One by one, Ma checked the three other stinky lumps of green-tinged flesh. They were all sound asleep.

"It's safe to go in!" said Rufus.

Even Bruno, Betty and Belinda, who were familiar with the troll lair, entered with some trepidation. Rufus and Polly needed extreme bravery and strength to set foot inside the stinky cave. Polly held her nose, worried that the stench would make her sick.

Rufus recognised Gobb Podgeleton. "That's the one that Bruno hit with his boomerang," he told Polly.

The Trolley family began emptying their sacks of supplies, and getting to work on the sleeping trolls. Ma bent over Gobb Podgeleton and removed two long pink ribbons from her bag. She bunched his knotted brown hair into two clumps, plaited each one and secured it with a ribbon. The ugly troll's hideous hair was now in pigtails!

The others found it difficult not to giggle as they saw the big, gruff troll wearing pigtails and little girl's hair accessories. Polly had to stuff her fingers in her mouth to stop herself laughing out loud.

Then, Ma pulled out the elasticated dress that she had made specially. It was mauve with white polka dots and a peach trim. She wrapped it around one half of Gobb. Then, very carefully, she began rolling him over, so that the dress wrapped around him.

The others held their breath. Would Gobb wake up?

Fortunately, he was a heavy sleeper. Ma fastened the dress together using the Velcro that she had stitched in to speed up the troll-dressing process.

When she had finished, Gobb looked hilarious – a big, fat, warty, grubby monster, in a pretty polka-dot dress. Nobody had ever seen anything like it. Ma turned to the rest of the group and smiled, proudly.

"That's awesome, Mum!" gasped Bruno. "He looks just like a little girl!"

"Except that he's knobbly, green and enormous!" said Polly, looking affronted.

"But he won't look green at dusk," Bruno

reminded her. "Once it starts to get dark, it's much harder to detect colours."

"And he won't look so tall in a bendy mirror," Rufus pointed out.

"True," agreed Polly.

And so, the six of them got to work dressing the horrible, sleeping trolls as pretty little girls. It was hard work. The two children needed help rolling the sleeping trolls into their costumes, but Bruno and his family were only too happy to help.

They dressed Boris Grimboil, a smelly, vulgar troll, in orange frilly socks and a cornflower blue pinafore. They dressed Mustyfur Wartface, a hard, muscular troll, in a tiara and pink skirt. They dressed a grisly, slimy troll in hot pants and a lacy vest.

Finally, all of the trolls in the main cave were wearing little girl costumes. The group looked at them and sniggered. They looked like the ugly sisters from *Cinderella,* but even more repugnant.

"But where are all the others?" asked Polly. "You said there were twelve and a half trolls and we've only dressed five."

"We haven't prepared Gunkfreak yet," said Rufus, shuddering.

"They'll be in other caves," explained

Bruno. "Follow me. I know where most of them sleep.

Bruno led the way, followed by the twins, Rufus and Polly. Ma took up the rear so that if any of the trolls in the first cave woke up, they'd just see a troll bottom disappearing into the tunnels and not the back of a tasty child.

As they moved forward, they started to smell a new putrid smell – definitely like a rotten egg with a sprout festering inside. "Gunkfreak!" recognised Rufus.

The ground started to rumble. They could hear roaring.

"It sounds like there's a dragon in here!" remarked Polly.

"Don't be silly Polly," said Rufus. "Dragons aren't real. It's a troll snoring, isn't it Bruno?"

Bruno nodded.

Eventually, the tunnel led into another large cave. It wasn't quite as big as the entrance hall but it was just as smelly. Seven lumps were asleep on the floor.

"That one's Gunkfreak," Rufus told Polly, pointing at the largest one.

"Then let's dress him first," she suggested.

Rufus was reluctant to go near Gunkfreak, his former captor. However, as soon as he saw the lime green tutu that Ma had made for him, he knew he was going to enjoy this one. Rufus took great pleasure in dressing the monster in the fluorescent tutu, a gold crown and the most enormous pink ballet shoes that he had ever seen. He looked ridiculous!

The others got to work dressing the remaining trolls. They worked quickly. The sooner they could get out of the cave, the better.

There were dangling earrings, sparkling bangles, knee length socks, pleated skirts and glittering vests.

Eventually, Polly whispered gleefully "We've finished!"

"No, we haven't," gulped Rufus. "Where is The Ogre of Uggle?"

"The Ogre of Uggle has his own cave," explained Bruno.

"But where is it?" asked Polly.

Bruno knew that The Ogre of Uggle's cave was the stinkiest place in the whole world – even stinkier than a tower of runny nappies seasoned with garlic. "I think it's best if you stay here," he told them.

"No chance," replied Polly, bravely. "We're in this together."

"All right," conceded Bruno, "but don't say you weren't warned!"

Ma led the way. The others followed, feeling even more nervous than they had when they first walked into the forest.

They followed a tunnel, which climbed upwards before taking a sharp dip downwards. Ma struggled with her crutches in some of the tighter spots, but she kept going. As they pressed forward, the stench got worse and worse.

"It's even worse than boys' trainers!" remarked Polly.

Suddenly, the ground beneath them rumbled.

"He must be awake!" cried Rufus.

"Not necessarily," Bruno replied. "He could just be snoring."

As they continued, the ground beneath their feet got softer.

"The Ogre of Uggle's cave is on the edge of the creek," explained Bruno.

"That explains the smell," said Polly.

"Narb," Bruno told her. "That's just his bottom."

"Urgh! It smells like cabbages rotting in stinky cheese sauce."

A little daylight began to illuminate the tunnel. They knew they must be close to the creek. Suddenly, Ma stopped. Bruno almost walked straight into her. Ma wobbled on her crutches.

"What is it?" he asked.

"I can see him!" she said, trembling.

"Is he asleep?"

"I think so."

Ma hobbled out of the tunnel and onto a ledge that hung above the spot where The Ogre of Uggle was sleeping. One by one, the others sneaked out to join her.

"Oh my!" cried Rufus.

"Yikes!" said Betty.

"That's revolting!" remarked Polly.

Rufus recognised The Ogre from their first meeting. He was almost twice as tall as Gunkfreak, twice as grubby and twice as smelly. He was lying in a thick layer of mud. A small opening led to mud flats. The air smelt as if somebody was steaming a poo – a poo pooped by somebody who ate only cabbages and stinky cheese.

I wish I'd brought my nose plugs, thought Rufus.

"He's already wearing some clothes," Polly said, pointing to his disgustingly dirty, white top hat, tattered orange bow tie and yellow y-fronts.

"He thinks they make him look important."

"They make him look ridiculous."

"I know!" laughed Bruno. "But the costume that Ma made him is even more hilarious."

"We have to go near *that*?" asked Polly, trembling.

"You can wait here. I'll do it!" offered Bruno, gallantly.

"No, *I'll* do it," insisted Rufus, getting competitive.

Bruno and Rufus lowered themselves down from the ledge. They landed in a thick layer of mud which made it hard for them to walk. Each time they lifted their feet the mud made a belching noise. *Belch!*

Slowly, they approached The Ogre. *Belch! Belch! Belch!* Fortunately, The Ogre was having a dream about bottom burps, so the belching did not disturb him.

"Pass us the sack, please?"

Ma dropped her sack down to them. Rufus caught it.

Rufus removed a ring of flowers from the sack. He crept closer to The Ogre. His hands shook as he removed The Ogre's top hat.

Suddenly, Rufus squealed – the hat was full of wriggling worms!

"Shush!" whispered Bruno.

"There are wriggling worms in here!"

hissed Rufus.

"That's where The Ogre keeps his snacks," explained Bruno.

"Worms are snacks?"

After Rufus got over the shock, he placed the hat aside and positioned the flowers on The Ogre's head, as gently as he could. Rufus could not risk The Ogre waking and seeing him in his den, particularly not when the mud around his ankles would make it so hard for him to run away. If The Ogre of Uggle awoke now, he would certainly eat Rufus! Then, he'd grab Polly and gobble her for dessert.

Bruno took The Ogre's costume from the bag. It was an enormous white, satin fairy dress! Rufus had seen smaller tents.

"Help me wrap this around him," whispered Bruno.

The two crept around The Ogre, wrapping the satin fabric around his gigantic, wobbly belly. Finally, they had covered every side of his body, except the side that was on the ground.

"Help me roll him over, please," asked Bruno.

Rufus walked around to join Bruno next to The Ogre's belly. *Belch. Belch. Belch.* Gently, they pressed their hands against him. Then, applying a little force at first, they tried to roll him. However, when a little force failed to do the job, they pushed harder. Then, when medium force failed to do the job, they pushed harder again. Suddenly, Rufus lost his footing and fell into the mud. *Splash.*

Bruno helped him up. *Belch, belch.*

"We'll all have to push together," Polly suggested.

"Don't come down here Polly," Rufus warned. "It's dangerous."

"Oh, stop treating me as if I'm fragile," scolded Polly, lowering herself down from the ledge without flinching.

Betty and Belinda followed her down. The mud nearly swamped their short legs. Ma wanted to join them but she couldn't climb with her bad leg. The youngsters all collected next to The Ogre of Uggle's enormous belly.

Betty and Belinda grabbed The Ogre's legs, Bruno and Rufus grabbed his body and Polly grabbed his head. Then, on the count of three, they all pushed. Betty pushed, Belinda pushed, Rufus pushed, Bruno pushed and Polly pushed. But The Ogre of Uggle still did not move.

"One more try!" ordered Bruno.

And so, Betty pushed, Belinda pushed, Rufus pushed, Bruno pushed and Polly pushed.

Suddenly, to their horror, The Ogre of

Uggle opened an eye!

"He's awake!" thought Rufus. "We're going to get caught, and then eaten alive!"

Chapter 13

The Really Silly Part

Quickly, the trolls stepped in front of Rufus and Polly, who ducked out of sight. By the time The Ogre of Uggle could focus his eyes, all he could see was the Super-Troll-Knobbly-Foot children.

"I thought you left," he yawned.

"We're back!" lied Ma, from the ledge.

"Back?" barked The Ogre, looking up at her. "What on earth are those in your hands?" he asked, pointing to the crutches.

"Sticks!" she fibbed. "For catching little children."

"Ooh!" said The Ogre, with interest.

"Living like humans didn't suit us," Bruno said, to keep up the deception.

The Ogre sat up, causing the whole cave to

143

shudder. "Of course it didn't suit you! We be trolls. We be supposed to be eating children, not pizzo and ships!"

"*Pizza* and *chips*," corrected Ma.

The Ogre rose. The ground rattled, causing a sound like thunder. Even dressed like a fairy, he was terrifying. "You think you know better than I, The Ogre of Uggle?" he bellowed, glaring at Ma.

"N ... narb ..." she stuttered.

"You think you can be leaving us and then be crawling back?"

"N ... n ..."

"You think you is welcome back after turning your back on us?"

"N ..."

"Be off with you!" he yelled at them all. "And don't be back here ever again!"

They were all more than happy to leave and never return. The Ogre of Uggle was a horrifying hunk of horror. However, they still hadn't fastened up his dress. If they didn't fasten the Velcro it could easily fall off. They needed to finish the job if they were to have any chance of killing him.

The Ogre glared at Bruno and the twins. None of them could sneak around behind him without him noticing.

Suddenly, Ma blew a raspberry, to distract The Ogre. The Ogre liked raspberries because they reminded him of bottom burps and The Ogre liked bottom burps.

Rufus saw his chance; he sneaked around to The Ogre's back. However, he could not reach the Velcro. He stepped onto a rock. Still, he could not reach the Velcro. Finally, he climbed onto an even higher rock. This allowed him to reach the Velcro fastenings on the fairy dress. He grabbed one side.

Ma noticed Rufus peeping out from behind The Ogre. She had to keep The Ogre occupied.

"School!" she said, suddenly.

"School?" asked The Ogre.

"I help you eat school!" she offered. She was lying, of course, but she had to hold his attention. If The Ogre of Uggle should notice that Rufus was behind him dressing him like a fairy, he would not only try to eat Rufus but would know that the Super-Troll-Knobbly-Foot family were plotting against him.

"And how be you doing that?" he bellowed.

Rufus managed to stick the prickly side of the Velcro to the fuzzy side. Betty quickly passed him the final touch to The Ogre's costume – fairy wings.

Ma had difficulty keeping a straight face as

Rufus attached fairy wings to The Ogre of Uggle's back. There he was, half troll, half giant, but dressed like Tinker Bell. He didn't look even remotely dainty but he did look entertaining.

Rufus sneaked back to join Polly, shielded by the good trolls. They all climbed back up onto the ledge, being careful not to expose the humans to The Ogre. Once on the ledge, they began filing into the tunnel.

"Where be you going?" demanded The Ogre.

"I ... er ... narb!" muttered Ma.

"Where be you going?" he repeated.

"Snooze," she lied, and hurried away into the tunnel.

"Come back here! I be wanting to hear your plan!" boomed The Ogre.

The Ogre of Uggle wanted to follow, but he was so fat and heavy that it took him a while to get up onto the ledge, by which time the speedy others had successfully scurried away.

* * *

The group hurried out of the cave and into the woods, as quickly as Ma's crutches would allow. They kept hurrying, through the woods, over the bumpy bridge, past the shops, past the playground and through the streets. They didn't stop hurrying until they got to Rufus's garden.

"Where be the den?" asked Ma, looking around and seeing only brambles, ferns and nettles at the bottom of the garden.

"Just wait and see!" Bruno told her.

Rufus pulled the branch that wasn't a branch. The small door woven from sticks and leaves opened. The twins were stunned.

"That's amazing!" exclaimed Betty.

"I can't be fitting in there!" laughed Ma.

Rufus pulled another branch that wasn't a branch. A second door opened next to the first.

"I've reinforced the ladder too," he told her.

They all crept inside and sat down on the upturned paint tubs and a special stool Rufus had made for Ma, using a barrel. At last a chance to collect their breath and reflect on their most recent escapade.

"Could have been worse," said Bruno.

"How?" asked Rufus.

"Well, we're still alive."

"Just."

Rufus passed around cups of lemonade. It was almost dusk and they needed to quench everybody's thirst before the next part of their plan.

"Shouldn't we get back into our human clothes?" suggested Bruno. "In case your parents see us dressed like this?"

"*The World's Next Top Singing Dog* is on. They won't come out here."

"Are you sure?"

"Positive, it's the series final. The judges have to decide which dog will get a recording contract."

Once he'd finished his lemonade, Bruno went outside and looked around for some large boulders. Each time he found one, he carried it to the riverside.

"How does he do that?" asked Polly, admiringly.

"Trolls are ridiculously strong," offered Rufus, who was equally impressed.

Bruno continued moving boulders until he had made a long line of them. Then, he stomped over to the pile of mirrors, grabbed the first one and lifted it clean off the ground.

"How does he do *that*?" asked Polly.

"Beats me, I could hardly lift one," Rufus told her.

Bruno propped the mirror against the first boulder. By the time the others had finished their lemonades, Bruno had almost finished assembling a wall of mirrors.

"Wow! That's amazing!" gasped Rufus. "Thanks Bruno."

Polly walked around to the front of the mirrors. She squealed with delight when she saw how short it made her look. "It works! It really works!" she cried.

Rufus looked at himself in the mirror and admired his small, distorted reflection. He found himself wondering, once again, where those mirrors had come from. How had they suddenly appeared in his garden?

"Now time for another really pongy part!" announced Polly. She disappeared inside the den and reappeared carrying one of the sealed sacks of shoes. She was just about to empty it onto the grass behind the mirrors when Rufus came running over to her.

"Here, use these!" he told her, offering her a pair of nose plugs. "You put them up your nostrils to block the smell."

"Have these been up your nose?" demanded Polly, looking concerned.

"No, they're new ones!" replied Rufus, indignantly. "What do you think I am? – disgusting or something?"

Then, he plucked the pair he'd previously used from his pocket and, unconcerned by his own dried-on snot, plopped them up his nose.

Polly emptied a sack full of stinky trainers into a pile on the lawn. Being enclosed in sacks had made them pong even more. Rufus and Bruno followed suit and emptied their bags. Even with nasal plugs, the two humans could tell that the shoe pile was the stinkiest man-made structure in the world. The pong was so bad that three slugs and a passing skunk fainted. A sparrow threw up in the flowerbed.

"How long will we have to wait?" wondered Polly.

"It won't be long," Bruno guessed. "Now that the shoes are out of the bags, their fragrance can reach its full potential. The bad trolls will detect it in no time."

"Well then, we should all climb to the top of my den and watch from there. It's much safer than being down here," suggested Rufus.

"We're perfectly safe down here. The trolls won't be able to cross the river," Bruno reminded him.

"Well, we'll get a better view from up there," explained Rufus. "And we'll be away from their line of sight. If the trolls see us peeping out from behind the mirrors, they might smell a rat."

"True," agreed Bruno.

"Now, where are your sisters?"

They looked around. Betty, Belinda and Ma were playing, actually *playing* in the pile of smelly shoes.

"Yuck! How could they?" asked Polly.

"We're trolls. We like the smell," Bruno reminded her. "To us, it's like rolling in chocolate marshmallows."

Polly sometimes forgot that the Trolley family were trolls. They had seemed most peculiar at first but were rapidly adapting to human conventions. She had never imagined herself liking a troll, but she thought Bruno was awesome.

"Come on everybody!" called Rufus. "It's almost dusk. The trolls will soon leave their caves and hurry this way. Let's get up onto the top of my den so that we can watch!"

"Yay!" sang the twins, dropping the shoes and scurrying towards the den. Ma, who was savouring a plimsoll, needed a little extra convincing.

"Come on, Mum!" called Bruno. "Don't you want to see Gunkfreak get what he deserves?"

Ma dropped the plimsoll, and hopped over to the den. She needed a little help climbing the ladder but soon joined the rest of them.

"They're coming!" cried Polly. "Listen!"

They all stopped talking and listened. A low rumble could be heard coming from the Fusty Forest. The rumbling got louder and louder. It sounded like a herd of elephants storming across a big bass drum. Instinctively, they all ducked down and then, slowly, they peeped up above the leafy wall surrounding the balcony.

"Why can't we see them yet?" asked Polly. It was starting to get dark but there was still enough light to see a troll clearly.

"Give them time," whispered Bruno.

The rumbling intensified and was joined by the sound of splintering wood. Finally, the trees on the opposite riverbank began to shake.

Suddenly, out popped Gobb in his mauve dress with white polka dots and a peach trim. His eyes were crazed and his lips were hungry, but his hair was pretty and his dress cute. They didn't know whether to laugh or tremble.

Then, another troll appeared from the trees. This one was a little hairier than Gobb. He wore a pinafore and striped tights.

Gobb turned to the second troll. "Did you be doing something different with yer hair?"

"I don't be thinking so. Why?"

"You be looking a bit ... well ... *pretty*!"

"Oh!" sung the other troll, blushing. "So be

you. Be that a new troll cloth?"

Gobb looked down at the dress. "Must be."

Polly giggled. "They really are thick, aren't they?" she whispered to Rufus. "If I woke up in somebody else's clothes, I'd want to know why!"

Suddenly, Gobb boomed "Hey!" He raised a hairy arm and pointed directly ahead of him at the mirror across the river.

The other troll followed his gaze. "Little girl!" he shouted.

They stood, mesmerised by their reflections in the specially positioned mirrors. Their reflections, of course, were much smaller than the trolls themselves, because they were looking into special bendy mirrors. And, because the trolls were wearing frilly dresses, their reflections looked rather a lot like little girls.

The troll with the stripy tights licked his lips and sung, "What a lovely *plump* little girl. So much meat on her bones!"

"Come here, little girl!" Gobb shouted at his own reflection.

"Come here, little girl!" echoed the other troll, at his similar reflection.

They stared at their mini-likenesses for a few moments longer, until suddenly Gobb took a few steps backwards. Then, he put his hands out to the side like two wings made from sausages.

"What be you doing?" asked the other troll.

"I be flying," he explained. "Just you watch!"

With that, Gobb rushed forward as fast as he could. Then, he leapt into the air, flapping his enormous arms.

Splash!

Gobb landed splat in the middle of the Muckygush.

He disappeared under the water.

The others watched, waiting for him to resurface but he did not. He was fat and heavy and sank like a potato stuffed with rocks. Gobb the troll was well and truly dead.

"It's working!" chortled Rufus, with glee. "Our plan is working!"

"It worked once," agreed Polly. "But surely the second troll won't be stupid enough to try and jump across the river now that he's seen Gobb fail."

Before Polly could finish speaking, the second troll took a few paces back. "Eeeeee!" he screeched as he ran forward with his mammoth arms out.

Then, *splat!*

The second troll fell into the river. Just like Gobb, he didn't resurface.

"Wow – stupid," observed Polly.

The hairy troll with the pinafore and striped tights was well and truly dead.

"Two down, ten-and-a-half to go," announced Rufus, excitedly.

It wasn't long before six more trolls appeared at the riverside. Just like their predecessors, they became mesmerised with their reflections. They started yelling excitedly.

"Pretty little girls!"

"Tasty little girls!"

"Meaty little girls!"

One of them sang a little song,

"Little girl, all pretty and smelly,

It's time for my tea, come into my belly!"

Then, all at once, the six trolls extended their arms, took a couple of steps backwards and then hurried forward. Each was certain that he would be able to make it across the river. Each was wrong.

Splash.

    Splash.

        Splash.

            Splash.

                Splash.

                    Splash.

Six trolls. Six leaps. Six splashes. And, not one troll made it to the bank. Rufus and his friends watched with glee. Over half of the bad trolls were well and truly dead.

"Our plan is working tremendously!" Rufus chuckled. "Only four more to go!"

"But don't forget The Ogre of Uggle," Bruno reminded him.

Rufus gulped.

Polly suddenly looked concerned.

"What's the matter?" asked Bruno.

"What if the next troll lands on top of one of the trolls that has already drowned? The dead trolls will make the river shallower. What if that means that the next troll doesn't go under?"

Rufus shook his head. "The currents in the Muckygush are strong. Those trolls will have been swept away already. Gobb Podgeleton will be almost at sea by now."

"That's if the crocodiles haven't gobbled him up first," Bruno reminded him. "Don't worry, Polly. Everything will be all right."

"I hope so."

Four more trolls lined up along the bank. Rufus recognised Gunkfreak, Tash, Boris Grimboil and Mustyfur Wartface. He watched intently, remembering how Gunkfreak had kidnapped and planned to eat him. The tables had turned.

The trolls stood on the bank admiring their reflections and remarking on how tasty the little girls looked.

"That one be dressed like a ballerina!" sung Gunkfreak, looking at his own reflection.

"My one has lovely socks," remarked Boris Grimboil.

"My one has a tiara!" commented Mustyfur Wartface.

"Why be my one having a snotty moustache?" asked Tash.

"May be a crusty caterpillar on her lip," Gunkfreak suggested.

"Of course!" said Tash, pleased with the explanation. Then, she yelled, "I be coming to get you!" And, of course, she put out her arms, ran forward and took a running jump.

Splash! Tash fell into the river.

Splash! Boris Grimboil fell into the river.

Splash! Mustyfur Wartface fell into the river.

Not one of them resurfaced. Three more trolls were well and truly dead.

However, Gunkfreak did not jump. He stood and watched his foolish kinsfolk with bemusement.

"Fools!" he bellowed.

"Oh no!" whispered Rufus. "He's figured it out! Gunkfreak, one of the scariest of all the trolls, has figured it out!"

They watched with terror as Gunkfreak scratched his head. He looked at his reflection and saw a little girl in a lime green tutu and pink ballet shoes, but he knew that something wasn't right.

Polly wondered if Gunkfreak had noticed that the supposed 'little girl' before him had horns. She wondered if he could detect that her skin had a faint greenish tinge. She wondered if he would see that the little girl was more knobbly and ugly that any other little girl he had ever seen.

Then, suddenly, Gunkfreak leapt into the air. He didn't run forwards like the others, but upwards. He wrapped his warty hands around a branch of the tree that hung over the river.

"No!" gasped Rufus.

Gunkfreak *was* cleverer than the others after all! He was going to swing himself across the river and eat them alive!

Chapter 14

The Really Scary Part

Rufus and his friends held their breath. Their hearts pounded inside them like trapped angry ferrets. If Gunkfreak made it across the river, they would all be in great danger.

But then, suddenly, they heard the sound of splintering wood. The branch gave way under Gunkfreak's enormous weight.

Splash!

Gunkfreak dropped into the Muckygush.

They watched …

… and they watched …

But Gunkfreak did not resurface.

Gunkfreak, one of the most dangerous trolls of all, the troll who had been plotting to attack the school, was well and truly dead.

The group cheered. Rufus gave Polly and then Bruno a high five. Before long, the group were all high-fiving each other. They grinned with delight.

They had dreamt up a plan – a bizarre, unlikely, dangerous and difficult plan – and it had worked! The school had been saved. The children of Sludgeside were safe.

"We did it!" cried Rufus.

"We saved the school!" rejoiced Polly.

"Look!" exclaimed Bruno, pointing at the river with delight.

A crocodile cruised past, the gold crown that Gunkfreak had been wearing on its head. It was licking its lips. A knobbly greenish beast that had gobbled many children had himself been gobbled up by a knobbly greenish beast.

But suddenly, the ground started rumbling again. This time, it felt as though they were standing on the back of a giant rhinoceros blowing its nose during the worst cold of its life. They were met with that stench of cabbages rotting in stinky cheese sauce.

"The Ogre of Uggle!" cried Bruno.

"Oh no!" screamed Rufus.

"Keep calm," said Polly. "He's half troll. That means that he's half-stupid. He'll run into the river just like all the other trolls. He's even heavier than Gunkfreak so he won't be able to swing from a tree."

"She's right," agreed Bruno. "We have nothing to fear."

Yet for some reason they were all scared – very scared indeed.

Just at that moment, The Ogre popped his head out between two large fir trees. He was still wearing the ring of daisies that Rufus had attached to his head. A daisy chain can take the edge off even the scariest sight. Polly found herself smirking a little.

As The Ogre stepped forward, the rest of his body appeared wearing the white, satin fairy dress that Ma had made especially. Polly sniggered.

He trotted around, trying to find the source of the stinky shoes smell. Then suddenly, he froze. He had seen his reflection in the mirror.

"Why isn't he smiling?" Polly asked. "He should think he's looking at a little girl."

"I don't know," admitted Rufus, worried.

"Perhaps he's too clever," suggested Bruno. "He is half-giant. Giants aren't known for their brains, but they are smarter than trolls."

However, suddenly The Ogre did smile. "What a pretty little girl!" he barked, staring at his reflection. "I do love to be eating pretty little girls! And the ones that dress like fairies taste the sweetest of all! It's suppertime!"

Then, he took a few steps backward.

"He's going to try and jump!" whispered Polly.

"He's going to fall in the river!" said Bruno, with glee.

The Ogre of Uggle threw his arms out like sausage-shaped wings.

He ran forward.

He leapt.

He hurtled through the air.

He landed.

The Ogre had made it across the river!

"Heck!" cried Rufus.

"How did he do that?" screamed Polly.

"It's because he's half giant," explained Bruno. "His legs are longer than the other trolls. He can jump further."

"Yikes!" cried Polly.

The Ogre of Uggle stood in front of the mirror. He reached out a giant sausage arm and tried to grab the little girl in front of him.

Smash!

The mirror shattered.

The Ogre cried out in frustration. He looked at the fragments of glass around him and realised that the little girl had been nothing more than an illusion. He had been duped!

The Ogre was furious. Who had done this to him? He looked around. He could definitely smell children. There must be a girl around here somewhere. He stomped towards the den, following his nose.

Being half-giant, The Ogre's eyes were at the level of the balcony. Polly ducked, but not before The Ogre had seen her. He tried to get up on tippy toes but he wobbled and fell over.

"Quick, run!" Bruno cried at Rufus and Polly. "Get away before he gets up again!"

"We're not leaving you!" Rufus replied.

"Go!" ordered Bruno. "The Ogre won't eat us – we're trolls. We taste like poo jam on burnt toast."

"Come on!" shouted Polly. She was already half way down the ladder. Rufus followed.

"Where are we going?" asked Rufus.

"Anywhere away from here!"

They exited the den using its emergency fireman's pole down to the lawn. Unfortunately, this left them less than three feet away from The Ogre of Uggle. They could see his eyes – he was looking straight at them!

The Ogre spotted Polly. She wasn't the littlest girl he'd ever seen but she certainly looked tasty. He dragged himself up onto his feet.

Polly screamed and froze.

Rufus grabbed her hand and tried to pull her away from The Ogre. Rufus was taller than Polly and could run much faster.

The Ogre of Uggle reached out a sausage arm. He tried to grab Polly by her ankle. The tips of his fingers clawed against her skin but he didn't manage to get hold of her.

Polly ran away, helped by Rufus. Her ankle stung.

But The Ogre of Uggle was half giant and every one of his strides was longer than four of theirs. He caught up with them in no time. He reached out. His hand was so big that he managed to grab Polly around the waist and hold her in his fist. He picked her up and held her at the level of his face. Polly could see his bogies – big, slimy and green as if a small collection of slugs had just crawled up his nostrils.

Polly screamed.

"Put her down!" yelled Rufus.

The Super-Troll-Knobbly-Foot family had assembled on the lawn.

"You grab his left foot!" Bruno shouted at Betty and Ma. "Belinda, you and me grab his right foot."

"And me?" asked Rufus.

"Run!" screamed Bruno.

But of course, Rufus could not run away, not when The Ogre of Uggle had his best friend captured and was about to eat her. He had to stay and see that she got away.

The Super-Troll-Knobbly-Foot family launched themselves on The Ogre's feet. The largest of them, Ma, reached only as high as The Ogre's bottom. The twins were barely up to his knees. They pushed and pulled at his ankles, hoping to unbalance him, but he stayed steady on his feet. Bruno bit The Ogre's foot.

"Ugh!" he cried. "Tastes just like cabbages, stinky cheese, poo jam *and* burnt toast all at once!" He spat on the grass.

"I be looking forwards to gobbling you all up!" The Ogre said to Polly.

"I'm poisonous!" she lied.

"That be a lie!" he shouted. "You think you can be tricking *me*? I am The Ogre of Uggle!"

"You're The Ogre of *Ugly* and you're a bully!" she cried.

The Ogre was fuming. "Right! That's it!" he shouted. "It be dinner time!"

The Super-Troll-Knobbly-Foot family tried with all their might to topple him over. Ma kicked his right foot while Bruno punched his left. But The Ogre of Uggle didn't even wobble. He opened his enormous mouth.

"This is it!" thought Rufus. "The Ogre of Uggle is going to eat my best friend."

The Ogre lifted Polly closer to his mouth. She could see his tonsils – like two oozing jellyfish. "This is it!" she thought. "He's going to gobble me all up!"

Chapter 15

Oily Pongbottom

The Ogre's teeth were full of cavities but they looked sharp. Bits of worm were caught in his gums. Polly closed her eyes, hoping that being eaten wouldn't hurt too much.

Then, suddenly, an arrow shot through the air and lodged in The Ogre of Uggle's cheek. He screamed in pain and dropped Polly on the grass.

Another arrow sliced the air and pierced The Ogre of Uggle in the right nostril. Finally, a third arrow stabbed him in the belly. The Ogre staggered backwards in shock. He tried to pull the arrows out of his tough skin but he was too stunned to co-ordinate his movements. He staggered backwards again. Then ...

SPLOSH!

The Ogre of Uggle fell backwards into the Muckygush.

The others watched, mouths open. They couldn't believe their luck – saved in the nick of time – *somehow*.

Rufus and Bruno rushed forward to where Polly was brushing herself off on the lawn.

"Are you okay?" they asked, in sync.

"Yes, I think I am!" she replied, standing up. "Is he definitely dead?"

The two boys crept cautiously toward the river and peered in. They waited and waited, but The Ogre did not resurface. Rufus noticed a very queasy-looking crocodile. It burped loudly, sending an impressive cloud of stench into the air. The boys smelt cabbages rotting in stinky blue cheese and they knew exactly what the crocodile had had for dinner – The Ogre of Uggle!

"Well and truly dead!" gulped Rufus.

"Where did that arrow come from?" asked Polly.

They looked around.

Suddenly Rufus saw a troll-shaped figure disappearing into the distance. "There!" he cried.

Ma grabbed her crutches and began

hurrying after it. She was getting pretty speedy but was no match for the mystery archer, who had full use of his legs.

"Non't!" she yelled. "N'again!"

"What is she saying?" asked Polly.

"Oh no you don't. You're not leaving us again!" translated Bruno.

"But why would she say that?" asked Rufus. "Does she know who the mystery archer is?"

They were all desperate to know who had saved the day. Why would he or she run away? They all followed Ma, who followed the mystery figure. Even Polly, who was a little bruised, jumped up and gave chase.

Eventually, the archer met the row of conifers that framed the garden. He pushed himself through the branches only to find a fence on the other side! He jumped to try to clear it, but Ma caught him by the ankles. He fell back onto the lawn. *Thud.*

The troll before them looked a lot like Bruno, but taller and with longer, crazier hair. He had a beard that didn't look as though it had been trimmed in five years.

"Marv!" shouted Ma.

"Marv?" asked Polly.

"Dad?" enquired Bruno.

"Dad?" echoed the twins.

"Marv the Magnificent?" asked Rufus.

"That's me!" he said, picking himself up of the lawn.

"Why were you running away?" asked Bruno, clearly hurt.

"So that Gunkfreak doesn't kill me!"

"But Gunkfreak can't kill you, he's dead!" explained Bruno.

"He is?" asked Marv, with great interest.

"Yarb, he just drowned in the river. Then, a crocodile gobbled him up," Bruno told him.

"Then it's safe for me to come out of hiding?"

"Why hiding?" demanded Ma.

"Because I shot Oily Pongbottom."

"Why?" asked Ma.

"I bet he had it coming," whispered Bruno.

"He was going to eat a little boy so I stunned him with an arrow."

"Wow!" gasped Rufus, remembering that night when he was five years, three-hundred and sixty-four days old.

"When Oily came around, he recognised my arrow," explained Marv.

"How?" asked Bruno.

"Because of the sausage carved on one side and the hippopotamus on the other," explained

Marv.

"Like my boomerang!" exclaimed Bruno.

"Dumbo!" cried Ma. "Got you caught!"

"Those are my signature carvings!" he protested. "But when Oily told The Ogre of Uggle what I had done, he was furious. He said he would get Gunkfreak to kill me."

"Gosh!"

"So I went into hiding."

Ma began smacking Marv with one of her crutches.

Bruno pulled her off. "Ma, what are you doing?"

"Ya left me with three kids!" she cried.

"I'm sorry," explained Marv. "It felt like saving the boy was the right thing to do at the time!"

"It was!" said Rufus, stepping forward.

Marv would recognise that red hair and those shiny blue eyes anywhere, even after five years. "Boy?" he asked, looking at him with deep curiosity.

"You saved *me*!" he said. He wrapped his arms around Marv the Magnificent. Then, he turned to the others. "Marv saved *me*!" he explained, with great delight. "He was the troll hunter who saved me when I was five years, three-hundred and sixty-four days old!"

"Troll hunter?" scoffed Ma. "He *be* a troll!"

"I am not like other trolls!" protested Marv. "I don't eat little boys."

"What happened to Oily Pongbottom?" asked Rufus.

"Nobody knows," Bruno told him. "Two years ago he said he was going on holiday and never came back."

"Do you think he ever will?" asked Rufus, alarmed.

"Who knows?" Bruno shrugged.

"I will be ready for him if he ever does!" declared Marv.

"Narb! No more heroics!" shouted Ma, angrily.

"You've learnt some new words!"

"Don't be avoiding the question!"

"But those troll are evil! Eating children is wrong."

"We know!" explained Bruno. "You taught us that and I've never even tasted human. But we've taken things even further."

"What do you mean?"

"We don't steal animals either."

"But how do you eat?"

"We pretend to be humans!"

"Humans?" asked Marv.

"Yarb! That way, the government helps Ma

with money for food," Bruno told him.

Marv looked thoughtful. Finally, he said, "Well, that won't do."

"But it's working. We're not hungry anymore and we're not stealing animals ..."

"I mean, getting money off the government won't do. I will get a job!"

"A job?"

"Yarb, a job."

"But what will you do?" asked Bruno, surprised.

"I'm sure I could put my brain to good use. I am the cleverest troll in the land."

Rufus and Polly were quiet. 'The cleverest troll in the land' wasn't much of a boast considering how stupid the rest of them were – or rather *had been*. They remembered that most of the trolls in Sludgeside were now dead.

"I be getting a job too!" broke in Ma, excitedly.

"Doing what?" asked Bruno, more rudely than he intended.

"Sewing!" she announced, proudly.

Bruno had to admit that, whilst Ma hadn't been the most employable woman in the world, she had become excellent with a sewing machine. "What a good idea!" he declared.

"We'll have to get a house!" suggested

Marv.

"We've got a house," said Bruno, proudly.

"Excellent! I've been living in the Sludgeside old folks' home for five years. I am looking forwards to sleeping somewhere comfortable."

"An old folks' home?"

"Yarb, in the cellar. It not been ideal, but I knew Gunkfreak would never find me there."

"Trolls hate old people," explained Bruno. "They get stuck in their teeth."

"Oh," said Rufus, flatly.

"Why didn't you go far way?" asked Bruno. "That would have been safer."

"I've been sneaking into forest to watch you and your sisters play."

"Wasn't that very dangerous?"

"Yarb, but it was the headlight of my day!"

"Highlight," corrected Rufus. Then he had a light-bulb moment. Suddenly, he felt he understood where the unexpected mirrors came from. "Did you bring us the mirrors?" he asked.

"Mirrors?" asked Marv. He looked totally mystified. He clearly knew nothing about any mirrors. Rufus was as puzzled as ever. Where had they come from?

"I'm hungry," said Marv. "Where is this

food you speak of?"

"At house," explained Ma.

"Why don't we go home and have a nice meal," suggested Bruno. "Rufus and Polly can come too, can't they Ma?"

"Yarb!" she said, with a big grin. "But no more dumb heroics," she told Marv.

"All the bad trolls are dead," Bruno whispered to his dad.

"Yarb," agreed Marv. "No more stupid heroics."

And so, Bruno, Rufus, Polly, Marv the Magnificent, Ma, Betty and Belinda headed to the Super-Troll-Knobbly-Foot house for a dinner of food bought from a supermarket.

Every bad troll in Sludgeside was now well and truly dead. Polly hadn't been eaten. The school had been saved. Marv the Magnificent had returned safely home. From now on, life would be much more ordinary.

"What's for dinner?" asked Marv.

Ma beamed a giant smile. "Scrubbing brush pie and paint stripper milkshake."

Epilogue

Marv the Magnificent began teaching Rufus all the tricks of troll hunting. If a bad troll ever set foot in Sludgeside again, Rufus would be waiting with many new skills and weapons – including the hippo bomb and the sausage slinger.

Polly became Rufus's chief plan maker. She had all sorts of zany ideas for catching bad trolls. With Bruno's help, she invented a troll tonic that you could give to trolls to make them hiccup. After drinking troll tonic, trolls would find it impossible to sneak up on children.

Bruno was still pretending to be human. His new friends had given him tips on how to look more realistic whilst at school. However, when they were alone he didn't bother with his hat, fake tan and bubble gum. His friends were happy for him to be himself.

Marv and Ma both got jobs, which meant they had more money to spend on their family. The twins tried cycling for the first time but, being built like potatoes filled with rocks, they wobbled and fell off so often that their parents took their bikes back and replaced them with scooters. However, being built like potatoes filled with rocks, they wobbled and still fell off. Their parents took back the scooters and replaced them with roller-skates. However, being built like potatoes filled with rocks, they wobbled and crashed. Eventually, their parents found the perfect present – a bouncy castle.

One day Mr Crimplemop asked Rufus to wait after class. The teacher was smiling, so Rufus assumed he wasn't in trouble.

"Teacher's pet!" scoffed Anita Grumblenose.

"Keen bean!" snorted Barry Blither.

Rufus ignored them. He knew that if it weren't for him and his friends, Anita and Barry would be troll dung, along with everybody else in the school.

The class filed out. "Sit down, please," Mr Crimplemop told Rufus.

Rufus took a seat next to the teacher's

desk.

Mr Crimplemop handed him back his homework – a long story called 'The Troll Trap'.

"Did you like it?" Rufus asked.

"It was excellent," he told him. "You must be very proud of it."

"I *am* pleased with it. But there's one loose end that I wasn't able to wrap up – one mystery that I couldn't explain."

"What's that?" asked Mr Crimplemop.

"The mirrors," he replied. "Where could they have come from?"

"Very puzzling," the teacher said, with a knowing sparkle in his eye. He took a swig from the mug that his Uncle Splendiferous had given him. "Very puzzling indeed."

About Rosen Trevithick

Rosen has written many best-selling books for adults. She has spent a lifetime writing stories for the children in her life. *The Troll Trap* is the first of those titles to be available for children everywhere.

She identifies as a child in adult's clothing and enjoys playing on swings, making clay trolls and collecting Playmobil people. She also enjoys swimming outdoors, hats with ears and eating chocolate. She dislikes house spiders, clearing up and troll dung.

Rosen was born in Cornwall and grew up on a creek. She studied at St Catherine's College, Oxford, before moving back to the West Country. She now lives on the south coast of Devon with two imaginary cats, dreaming about getting a real one.

About Katie W. Stewart

Katie W Stewart was born in Lancashire, England and emigrated with her family to Australia as a child. She has worked as an archaeologist, ethnohistorian and teacher, but these days she works as a Library Assistant and relief teacher at a school in country Western Australia. She is married to a farmer and has three children aged 9-19 as well as a small menagerie of pets. In her spare time, she writes fantasy novels, illustrates books, paints pet portraits and plays celtic harp and guitar.

www.SmellyTrolls.co.uk

Made in the USA
Charleston, SC
28 March 2013